*Christmas in Ireland*

# *Christmas in Ireland*

## Kaylee O'Shay, Irish Dancer

### Rod Vick

Laikituk Creek Publishing

# *Christmas in Ireland*
## Kaylee O'Shay, Irish Dancer

Laikituk Creek Publishing
North Prairie, Wisconsin

ISBN-13: 978-0-6924537-4-2
ISBN-10: 0-6924537-4-1

For Myra.

# What readers are saying about the Kaylee O'Shay series...

*Author Rod Vick offers motivational and inspiring lessons. Finally...dancers can identify with their own hero.*

Review in *Irish Dance & Culture Magazine* on *Green Storm*

*I loved it. I think it's (Fire & Metal) the best Kaylee book yet. Your book has everything!*

Brenna Briggs, author of Liffey Rivers series

*I think the concept and book are brilliant. There's been a glaring hole that your book series is filling.*

Jeff Winke, author of the <u>PR Idea Book</u> and father of a Riverdancer, on *Kaylee's Choice*

*My daughter was up reading the book all night.*

Mary Reese, mother of an Irish dancer

*Here is a book every aspiring dancer should read.*

*Hornpipe* magazine on *Kaylee's Choice*

*I just finished reading Kaylee's Choice, and I must tell you I'm eagerly awaiting the next book. It's not just about Irish dancing, but about caring, sacrifice, sportsmanship and everyday living—things all children need to know.*

*Pat Dilley, grandmother*

*I hope many of the dancers that compete are inspired as much as I am while I read these books.*

Chelsea Williams, Irish dancer

*I've just finished it (Kaylee's Choice) and wanted to say how amazing it was. It's been passed to my mom to read and I'm anxiously awaiting the next one.*

Emily Fondren, preliminary champs dancer

## Books by Rod Vick

*Christmas in Ireland*

*The Irish Witch's Dress*
*The Irish Witch's Tiara*
*Dancer in the Painted Mask*
*Dance of Time*
*Isle of Green Fire*
*Winds of Ireland*
*The Secret Ceili*
*Fire & Metal*
*Green Storm*
*Kaylee's Choice*

For more information, visit
www.kayleeoshay.com

*Dance till your legs grow numb,*
*Till you can't stop and you've become*
*A dance machine who runs on dreams,*
*Who won't stop dancing till all is seen*
*Through a dancer's eyes and a dancer's view.*
*Don't stop dancing till your time is through.*

- Alicia Strackbein

# One

She moved across the wooden stage, a whirl of navy and gold, precise as machinery, as elegant as wind. To her left, a dancer bobbed like a scarlet hummingbird, occasionally drawing near or even crossing her path, then flitting away to the opposite corner. Eighteen girls in brightly-colored school dresses stood waiting their turns along the back edge of the platform.

This was love. This was life. This, Kaylee O'Shay decided, was where she belonged.

A long-haired woman in her twenties fiddled joyfully from a chair at one corner of the ankle-high plywood stage, and the music seemed to lift Kaylee closer to Olympus than earth. At a table directly in front of both dancers sat the judge, an older, stern-faced woman who occasionally jotted notes onto the score sheet in front of her.

*Tip lift, tip lift, one-two hop back . . .*

For the first time in months, Kaylee felt real joy as she danced. She realized now that she had put too much pressure on herself at her previous two feiseanna—the name for Irish dance competitions. At that, her family had planned to move, and Kaylee had wanted to earn first places in all of her Novice-level dances before switching to a new dance school and suffering through a mandatory six-month waiting period prior to resuming competition. She had felt the pressure intensely and had not enjoyed her dancing, which normally was the most important thing in her life. Consequently, she had placed miserably.

Now, however, her father had gotten a new job and there would be no move, no new dance school, no six months of waiting. Once again, she could dance for the pure joy of it.

Today, she felt it. Today, she knew everything was clicking.

*Tip switch one-two cut, one-two hop, bang . . .*

Then, she stopped—so suddenly one might have thought she was an arrow that had been shot straight down into the stage. So did the much taller girl in the red dress, and both now bowed to the judge and musician as two girls from the line behind them began their steps while the music continued uninterrupted.

Kaylee and the other girl returned to the line, where they would stand at attention until all twenty dancers had finished. She could not keep a smile from her lips, nor could she keep from her mind the word that best seemed to describe how she felt:

*Awesome!*

When the dance concluded, she filed away from the stage with the others, and the next age group replaced them along the back side. As they moved past the rows of chairs set up for spectators near stage seven, a hand hooked her left elbow and Caitlin Hubbard, her best friend at Trean Gaoth Academy of Irish Dance, pulled her along even faster.

"You looked great out there!" squealed Caitlin.

"So did you," said Kaylee, breaking into a broad smile now that they were free of the judge's scrutiny.

Caitlin, a slim, chestnut-haired girl with large eyes, shrugged. "I've got to get up on my toes more." Then she smiled broadly. "But you were really on."

The two had competed against each other in the just-finished hornpipe. Sometimes they were spared this uncomfortable ritual. If the age groups were particularly large, they often were split into two smaller competition categories with the chance that Kaylee might land in one and Caitlin in the other. Today, however, the friends had gone head-to-head.

Now an arm slipped itself around her right elbow, and Kaylee turned to see Jackie Kizobu, her best friend from soccer, whose long, black hair and striking Asian features could not have been more different from Kaylee's freckles and rusty-blonde mop. Rarely did Kaylee have both of her best friends together in one place, since they lived in different towns and attended different schools. But then, today was a special day.

"People must dance better on their birthday!" said Jackie. "Zizzers, you just rocked everyone off the stage!"

Kaylee blushed. "Thanks. But it's not my birthday."

"It's the day of your birthday *party*, and that's good enough!" replied Jackie.

Kaylee's thirteenth birthday had actually occurred three weeks earlier in May, but there had been no time for a party, what with the bustle of activity that normally accompanies the end of the school year. As Kaylee's mother had studied at the calendar, she noticed that June looked pretty full as well.

"Why not just have the party at a feis?" Kaylee's Grandma Birdsall had suggested one evening at the dinner table. "You could rent a room at the Chicago hotel where the competition is being held and stay the night!"

Kaylee thought it sounded like a great idea. She and her friends from dance could go swimming, have cake and pizza and even a sleepover after the Saturday feis had been completed.

At first, there had been all sorts of objections from Mrs. O'Shay over how this would simply not work out. However, after Kaylee pointed out that most of her friends would already be at the feis, and that they could take Jackie—who was not a dancer—along with them, her mother's resolve began to weaken.

Mrs. O'Shay bit her lip, though, when considering the cost of a Chicago hotel room. This time, her father rode to the rescue.

"We can afford one night," he said. "Now that I've started the new job, and you're teaching classes at the fabric store, we've got a bit more money coming in. How often does our little girl become a teenager?"

"It had better not be more than once, or we'll be bankrupt," said Mrs. O'Shay, sensing that the battle had already been decided.

Then Kaylee had flashed her mother a wide, surrounded-by-freckles smile and victory was complete.

Kaylee and Caitlin had just completed the second of their two hard shoe dances, which featured exciting and gunshot-loud footwork. The remaining two dances would require them to wear their soft shoes, called ghillies. "I think we've got a break now before we dance again," said Kaylee.

"Great, because I'm starving!" cried Jackie, realizing that it was almost noon. "My dad said all there'd be to eat at an Irish dance competition would be boiled potatoes. I hope he was joking."

The three girls ran to the back of the hotel ballroom where dozens of families had camped out on blankets and folding chairs, preparing for or resting between dances. There they found Mrs. O'Shay and Mrs. Hubbard.

"You both looked so good," said Mrs. O'Shay.

"And beautiful," added Mrs. Hubbard.

"You look lovely, too, Jackie," added Grandma Birdsall, sitting in a comfortable camping chair, sewing away on something plaid.

"We want money," said Caitlin. "For food."

"Please?" added Kaylee.

"But I brought peanut butter and jelly," said Mrs. O'Shay, indicating a small cooler. However, her daughter's pleading eyes ultimately opened her purse. Caitlin already had money in her hand, and both mothers sighed as their daughters turned to escape.

Then: "Wait!" It was Caitlin's mother. She pointed to their dresses. "Smocks!"

The two dancers groaned, but dug the navy-blue smocks out of their garment bags and slipped them on so that no food would stain their expensive dresses. As Kaylee prepared to zip shut the pouch on her dress bag, she sensed that something was missing.

"Where are my ghillies?"

Mrs. O'Shay bent to look. "Aren't they right in your bag?"

Kaylee moved her hand back and forth, displacing mashed-up socks, a hairbrush, a plastic bag containing sock glue and other items essential to the well-armed dancer. "I don't see them!"

"I'm sure they're in there somewhere," said Mrs. O'Shay casually. "I double-checked before we left this morning. Go eat. We'll dig them out later."

The three needed no more prompting and scurried off toward the vendors. They wound through the crowd at the back of the ballroom and emerged into a wide hallway. Several other smaller rooms opened off of this, some containing a single temporary stage while others boasted two or three. Mrs. Hubbard had informed the girls that more than 1,300 dancers would be competing on nine separate stages.

The hallway was as crowded as the ballroom, filled with dancers in brightly-colored school dresses or vibrantly sparkling solo costumes. Parents, grandparents and other spectators also jammed the hall. The three friends headed to the right and emerged into a wider lobby where vendors had set up tables from which they sold t-shirts, Irish jewelry, Celtic music CDs and, of course, food.

"Over there," pointed Jackie, who spoke as though she were mere moments from starvation, and they hurried into a line that promised choices such as hot dogs, turkey wraps and soft pretzels.

Jackie and Caitlin purchased hot dogs, nachos and soft drinks, while Kaylee simply chose a soft pretzel.

"I don't want to eat too much now," she said. "I'm saving room for the cake and pizza later."

"I prefer to gorge myself at every opportunity," said Jackie, which caused the other two girls to exchange a look. Jackie Kizobu appeared to have only slightly more body fat than the skeleton in Mr. Peterson's science classroom at Kennedy Park Middle School.

As they returned to the camping area, Kaylee went over the day's schedule for the twentieth time. "Once the last group has danced and we find out how everyone placed, we'll meet in the main lobby. Then we'll go up to the room, change and go swimming!"

She could hardly believe what a wonderful day it was turning out to be. Not only was she doing her favorite thing in the world—Irish dance—but her best friends were all here and the evening promised a party and presents and an overnight stay in a hotel. Could the day get any better?

"Did you check to see how you placed?" asked Mrs. Hubbard. The results were posted near the main lobby about half an hour after each dance had finished, and the top three finishers received gold, silver or bronze medallions.

Caitlin shook her head. "We're waiting. It'll be more exciting that way." Then she paused thoughtfully. "I hope."

Kaylee and Caitlin both danced at the Novice level. Dancers usually started their competitive careers in the Beginner category, and after earning top-three finishes in their routines, moved to Advanced Beginner. More top-three finishes moved them into the Novice category. However, in Novice, the requirements were more daunting. Not only were the dancers more polished and athletic, one needed to earn a first-place in order to move up to the Open category in a dance.

But a first-place in Novice had another benefit.

Once a dancer earned a gold medal in Novice, she qualified for her solo dress. Prior to that, dancers wore their school dresses for feiseanna. Kaylee's school dress was beautiful, navy-blue and gold, and on the cape, a dove rose above a stylized gust of wind, surrounded by a wreath of Celtic knot. Of all her possessions, Kaylee loved her school dress more than anything—mostly because it had been made by her Grandma Birdsall when her family could not afford to pay for a new dress.

Even so, a solo dress was . . . well, it was the goal of every Irish dancer to qualify for one. It meant you were a member of an elite group whose dance skills had advanced to a higher level. It meant you could pick a dress that fit your unique personality, and most were full of color and sparkles and imagination—no two in the world exactly alike. Kaylee and Caitlin talked about earning their solo dresses all the time.

"Mine's going to be red," Caitlin often told her friend. "With lots of silver and blue sparkles!"

Kaylee wanted one just as desperately, but she often had a difficult time imagining that her solo dress would match her dream. "Mine will be whatever my family can afford."

Caitlin sat on a folding stool that kept the back of her dress from being crushed. Mrs. O'Shay pulled her nose out of Kaylee's garment bag, her face fraught with worry. "Honey, I still can't find your ghillies."

Caitlin's mother checked her wristwatch. "Their first soft shoe dance will be coming up soon." Then an idea seemed to come to her. "Do you suppose they're in the van?" They had ridden to Chicago in the Hubbard van.

Mrs. O'Shay decided that they might as well check and instructed the three girls to scour the camp site while they were gone.

A thorough search turned up nothing.  When the mothers reappeared, they were empty-handed, too.

"I *know* they were in that bag!" said Mrs. O'Shay anxiously.

Kaylee knew her mother was right.  Bethany O'Shay always revved herself into an ultra-paranoid state before they left for a feis, checking to see that no essential would be forgotten.

Mrs. Hubbard glanced at her watch again, nervously.  "We've got to get the girls over to the stage for check-in."

"You go," said Mrs. O'Shay.  "We'll keep looking."

"But Mom, we've looked *everywhere!*"

They looked everywhere again.  Jackie even looked underneath bags on nearby blankets, just in case— generating troubled looks from their owners in the process.  Grandma Birdsall looked in her sewing bag.

"Maybe somebody stole them!" suggested Jackie.

Kaylee shook her head.  Why would anyone steal her old ghillies?  Every dancer already had her own pair, and they were probably in better shape than hers.  And Kaylee had never known Irish dancers to steal things from each other.

As time evaporated, Mrs. O'Shay bombarded her daughter with the expected, frantic laundry list of questions.  Did you take the dress bag anywhere?  You're sure you didn't take the ghillies to the stage with you?  Did you take them out and set them on the blanket?  Are you sure you didn't remove them back at home before we left?

They were interrupted by Mrs. Hubbard who had hurried back from the stage.  "They're lining up the dancers for the slip jig!"

Mrs. O'Shay sighed in frustration and looked toward her daughter. "I'm sorry, honey, but it looks like you're going to miss your dance!"

This could not be happening, thought Kaylee. Not on this perfect day.

Not on the day of her birthday party.

But as she looked toward the stage at the back of the room, she saw her friend Caitlin lined up along the far edge with twenty other dancers.

And then, the music started without her.

# *Two*

"Happy birthday to you!"

The chorus of voices echoed off the sea-green tiled walls surrounding the hotel swimming pool, and in the middle of the cacophony sat Kaylee O'Shay.

Mrs. O'Shay snapped a photograph as her daughter blew out twelve of the thirteen candles.

Jackie laughed, pointing to the one still burning. "Kaylee has a boyfriend!"

The other six swimsuit-clad girls laughed, sounding like sixty as their voices reverberated off the tile. "Who'd go out with her?" asked Caitlin with a conspiratorial grin.

Kaylee stuck out her tongue. Mrs. O'Shay snapped another picture.

"I don't know," said Jackie in answer to Caitlin's question. "Maybe . . . Michael Black?"

Flash! Mrs. O'Shay caught the group in mid-ooh!

"I don't like Michael Black." Kaylee made a face to bolster the lie. Every girl at Kennedy Park Middle School liked Michael Black, the cutest boy in eighth grade. Not that it mattered. "In case you've forgotten, he's already going with someone."

"SomeTHING," grunted Jackie.

They all laughed and Mrs. O'Shay stepped in to serve the cake set atop a round patio table on one end of the pool room. A dozen other guests of various ages splashed in the pool or lounged in the hot tub, apparently oblivious to the celebration.

This was the first time all of her closest friends had been in the same place at the same time, Kaylee observed as Mrs. Hubbard scooped ice cream onto each cake slice before passing it along. Grandma Birdsall, who lived in the spare bedroom of the O'Shay house back in Rosemary, Wisconsin, had decorated the cake top with a beautiful frosting ghillie. She proudly added a plastic spoon to each plate as it passed her. Kaylee's father and her twelve-year-old brother, Will, had opted to miss the festivities in favor of a weekend soccer camp. She wondered what would happen if there were a soccer camp on her wedding day, which somehow conjured an image of Michael Black—an image she quickly pushed out of her head.

"I've got Kaylee's boyfriend!" sang April Lee, carrying a paper plate bearing the cake slice with the still-burning candle. Kaylee wondered how April, who danced for Trean Gaoth Academy with Kaylee, had gotten away with playing with fire in front of two adults to whom anything sharper than a baseball, hotter than tap water or riskier to operate than a toaster might represent an imminent and lethal threat. Any moment, she expected to hear her mother's voice: *Blow out that candle before someone loses an eye!*

"I've got her boyfriend's girlfriend!" cried Jackie, who carried a paper plate containing a slightly soggy, crumpled-up napkin. She dropped it ceremoniously into a nearby trash container, waving to it as the napkin disappeared. "Bye-bye, Brittany!"

Everyone laughed, and Mrs. O'Shay frowned her disapproval. "It's not nice to make fun of people who aren't here."

"Yeah, Kaylee," said Jackie, whose straight black hair and dark eyes usually made her seem mysterious and beautiful. Right now, however, her entire face was contorted in gleeful wickedness. "You should have invited Brittany so we could make fun of her in person."

Mrs. O'Shay passed out more cake and shook her head. "Now Jackie . . ."

"But Mrs. O'Shay, Brittany deserves it!" Jackie interrupted. "All those years when Kaylee and I played on the soccer team with her, she made mean comments to us every day. It was torture! I'm traumatized, possibly for life!"

Mrs. O'Shay gave Jackie an especially large piece of cake. "Maybe this will help you deal with your trauma."

It was true, thought Kaylee. Not about being traumatized for life, but the rest of it. Kaylee, Jackie and Brittany had all been members of the Green Storm soccer team from age five until Kaylee had quit two years ago to devote more time to Irish dance. In those six years, she could not remember one day that Brittany had not done or said something nasty to her.

There was the time Brittany broke Kaylee's leg in a soccer game. She had deliberately collided with Kaylee in order to steal the ball from her own teammate!

And the time Brittany stole Kaylee's Irish dance dress at the school talent show. Luckily Kaylee had found the dress after the show—hidden under an old canvas drop cloth.

And the time Brittany dumped puree of school lunch leftovers into the vent holes in Kaylee's locker, saturating her books, papers and other personal possessions. In all fairness, Kaylee *had* dumped puree of school lunch leftovers on Brittany's *head* first.

And the countless times that Brittany had voiced her opinion that Kaylee was the worst soccer player on the team.

What made it even worse was that Brittany was the *best* player on the soccer team—and her boyfriend was the cutest guy in the school.

But all of Brittany's previous crimes against humanity seemed trivial compared to what she had done today . . .

"Open the presents!" shouted Jackie, bouncing happily in her seat, apparently validating Mrs. O'Shay's theory about cake as a treatment for trauma.

Everyone crowded around the plastic table as Meghan O'Connell, another girl from Kaylee's dance school, passed her a colorful gift bag. Kaylee found the soundtrack to *Isle of Green Fire*—her favorite musical—which chronicled the volatile history of Ireland in powerful dance. Next she opened April's gift, a book about a girl training her horse to compete in a one hundred-mile race.

Kaylee hugged April and then sighed. "I love horses!"

April smiled. "I looked everywhere for books about Irish dancers, but all I could find were boring history books and stuff."

A tall girl, Hannah, pushed a gift across the coffee table toward Kaylee. "It's from me and Jordi!" she said proudly, inclining her head toward the smiling shorter girl next to her. The two girls had met Kaylee at a feis in Milwaukee. It was supposed to have been Kaylee's first competition, but her leg had been in a cast—thanks to Brittany. Jordi and Hannah, who danced for the enormous Golden Academy, had offered to help Kaylee carry out her plan to cut off the cast so she would not miss her first feis.

Ultimately, Kaylee had chickened out.

"We picked it out together!" said Hannah as Kaylee tore at the uneven wrapping.

"From the Golden Academy gift shop!" added Jordi.

Kaylee smiled. Golden Academy: probably the only Irish dance school in the world that had its own gift shop. Inside she found an adorable golden bear, all soft and squishy. It was wearing a tiny white t-shirt with the words GOLDEN ACADEMY on the front. *We'll have to lose the t-shirt*, thought Kaylee. But the bear itself would be in her arms when she fell asleep that night.

Golden Academy had more than a thousand dancers, compared to Trean Gaoth's fewer than three hundred. Golden dancers always seemed to win the big awards, and their dance studio looked like a health club for the rich and famous. Some people held the opinion that Golden Academy dancers were stuck-up, and Kaylee had felt that way at first—until she had actually *met* some of them. After meeting Jordi and Hannah, she realized that it did not matter what school you danced for. Dancers everywhere liked to compete, make friends and have fun.

Except for Brittany. Her mission in life seemed to be doing anything that made herself look good or made someone else feel bad. What she had done at the feis today was just one more example, and even now, Kaylee could not believe that one dancer would do such a thing to another.

Jackie's voice interrupted Kaylee's thoughts. "Open mine next!"

Jackie's present looked like a telescope, but when Kaylee picked up the package, it was obvious that a poster was wrapped up inside. Kaylee tore through the paper and unrolled the gift to reveal Angelo Zizzo, the Italian soccer star, muscles rippling, long hair flying in all directions, kicking a soccer ball past a hapless defender. Jackie had devoted a whole wall of her bedroom to various Angelo Zizzo posters.

"I realized," said Jackie, "that you really had everything a girl could want *except* an Angelo Zizzo poster."

Then Kaylee noticed something clipped to the bottom of the poster.

"It's a gift certificate for that ice cream shop in downtown Rosemary," Jackie explained. "The next time Brittany Hall does something mean to you, call me, and we can both go drown our sorrows in cookie dough!"

"Brittany Hall!"

The way Jordi had said the word made Kaylee glance around the room apprehensively, wondering whether her nemesis had walked through the doorway. Then Kaylee saw the surprise on Jordi's face as she repeated the name.

"Brittany Hall!   That's the Brittany you were talking about?"

Kaylee nodded.

Hannah looked at Jordi, her eyes wide, astonished. "Doesn't she dance for Golden Academy?"

Kaylee now realized that she had probably never told Jordi and Hannah all the Brittany stories, nor had she mentioned her last name.   Kaylee—with narrative help from Jackie and Caitlin—offered up a few tales of Brittany's misdeeds.

"She's a really good dancer!" said Hannah.    "I wonder why she's so mean to you?"

Kaylee had often wondered that same thing.    It could not be jealousy, Kaylee reasoned.    Soccer, Irish dance, getting cute boys to like her . . . Brittany was better than Kaylee at everything.

Caitlin piped in with an answer.    "I think it's because all the girls—" She stopped suddenly, and Kaylee understood why.    Caitlin had always despised Golden Academy--their bigness, their beautiful dance studio, their success.    With a smug look on her face, Caitlin had been about to make a disparaging remark about the girls at Golden, probably something like, "I think it's because all the girls at Golden are mega-snobs!"    Then, halfway through her comment, Caitlin had remembered that Hannah and Jordi were Golden dancers.    Her eyes darted back and forth, and she mouthed the air wordlessly.    Finally, a triumphant light appeared in her eyes and she continued.    "—all the girls on Kaylee's old soccer team— except Jackie, of course—were jealous because Kaylee's dad was the coach."

This seemed to satisfy Hannah, although Kaylee could not see how it made much sense at all.

"And she's the one who stole your shoes today?" asked Jordi.

Kaylee nodded, still finding the whole episode difficult to believe.    She had searched frantically for the ghillies, and then her first soft shoe dance, the slip jig, had started.    Afterwards she had pleaded with her mother to buy her another pair of ghillies so that she could dance her reel.

"They're very expensive," Mrs. O'Shay had explained, trying to be patient, yet feeling her daughter's hurt. "We can't afford to buy new shoes, especially if you simply left them home by accident."

Kaylee, however, knew she had not left them at home. She knew she had brought them to the feis.

Then the reel had been danced without her. What had started out as such a great day had deteriorated into an awful one. Being an Irish dancer and not being able to dance was one of the worst things in the world, like a jockey watching other people ride around the track or a gymnast sitting in the stands while all her friends tumbled and flipped their ways to the medal podium.

They had searched everything and everywhere again after that, but the damage had already been done. Half her dances—gone! Suddenly her awful day had plunged into the Just Plain Miserable Zone.

Mrs. O'Shay had been beside herself. "I'm going to check the van one more time." Off she had gone with Mrs. Hubbard and Grandma Birdsall in tow.

Caitlin returned from dancing her section of the reel and gave Kaylee a hug. "Sorry," she said demurely.

Kaylee had shrugged in resignation. "Oh well. There will be other feises." But inside she had felt a big, heavy, uncomfortable knot of frustration.

"Are we going to have cake now?" Jackie had asked.

This had made Kaylee smile, breaking the black spell just a bit. "We have to check the results to see if we placed."

The three had wandered to the hallway where large sheets of paper had been taped to the walls. Columns were labeled to indicate the age and skill level.

Dancers wore numbers around their waists, attached using a strand of ribbon. If a dancer's number appeared in one of the columns next to the dance, that meant she had earned a gold, silver or bronze medal. Before they could find their own dances, however, Kaylee felt someone tap her shoulder. She turned and her mouth fell open in shock. Heather Chandler, Brittany Hall's creepy toady and best friend stood facing her. But Heather was not a dancer, and Kaylee had never previously seen her at a feis. Before Kaylee could fully process this image of such an awful apparition in such a wonderful place, Heather thrust out a hand bearing a pair of ghillies.

"Here!"

Kaylee gasped. "My ghillies! But—"

Heather's lip curled as she spoke. "How old *are* these things? Can't you afford a pair made in this century?"

Kaylee looked at the shoes, then back at Heather, her eyes still wide with disbelief. "Where did you find them?"

Heather sneered as if addressing an earthworm. "I didn't find them. Brittany left her shoes in the car, which is way across the street in the parking garage. You weren't around at the time, but Brittany's dance was coming up, so I borrowed your shoes. As it turns out, you and Brittany are exactly the same size!"

Kaylee sputtered unevenly as she talked. "But you didn't even ask! You just took them! And I missed two dances!"

Heather shrugged. "So what? You're just a Novice dancer. It's not like the dances at *that* level are important. You're not in PC like Brittany." PC—Preliminary Champion—was a step higher than Open Prizewinner and was the second highest competitive category in all of Irish dance.

"Every level is important!" cried Caitlin. "But I don't suppose someone like you with your limited knowledge of dance—"

"Or limited brain power," added Jackie.

"—would understand!" concluded Caitlin.

Heather laughed a bitter molecule of laughter. "Whatever. I'd stay and talk, but I don't speak *Loser*. And they're just about ready to announce the PC results!" With that, she dropped the ghillies on the floor in front of Kaylee, who stooped to picked them up as Heather flounced away.

Kaylee stared after Heather. "How can somebody be such a complete—"

Jackie waited for it and then frowned. "Aren't you going to say it?"

Kaylee sighed. "I promised myself that I'd never swear at a feis. They're too special."

Jackie watched Heather disappear into the crowd and then turned back to Kaylee. "Do you mind if *I* say it?" She said it three times, though no one heard but Kaylee and Caitlin.

Then a voice boomed from nearby speakers and the PC results were announced. Kaylee scanned the crowd and found Brittany, offering a high-five as Heather rejoined her. The self-satisfied look on her face seemed to say, *Let's get on with it! Just give me my trophy so I can get out of here!*

But then a curious thing happened. As their names were called, girls in beautiful solo dresses paraded next to a table on which the enormous trophies had been set. Tenth place. Fifth place. Third, second, first. Brittany's name was not announced. Kaylee saw her face droop momentarily in surprise, but a moment later it had twisted into a pouting, toxic mask.

"She didn't place!" said Caitlin, whose shock prevented her from making any sort of mocking comment.

It did not prevent Jackie. "Isn't that just too bad? Poor baby!"

The three turned toward the charts where the other results were posted, but after only a few steps, Kaylee heard her name—or at least a version of it.

"O'Shrimp!"

It was Heather again. "Thanks a lot!" she called menacingly.

Kaylee's eyes widened. "What did I do?"

Heather stepped closer, her eyes full of rage. "Your loser shoes cost Brittany a trophy!"

Kaylee gasped, though it almost came out as a laugh. "You're blaming my shoes?"

"I should have figured they'd be bad luck!" Heather continued mercilessly. "Look who owns them! The Midget Queen of the Losers!" Then she whirled and disappeared, presumably following in whichever direction her evil bookend had gone.

"Hey!" called Caitlin, pointing toward the charts as the Heather storm cleared. "Take a look at this!"

Kaylee moved close to her friend, who stood pressed against a yellow rope that kept spectators a reasonable distance from the results boards. Caitlin pointed near the top. Kaylee found the columns for her reel and slip jig, the dances she had missed.

"I won't be placing in those today. That's for sure."

Caitlin smiled. "No, not in your soft shoes. But look at the hornpipe!"

Kaylee saw it finally. First place.

"I did it! I earned my solo dress!"

"Happy birthday!" beamed Jackie.

"And I got first in my slip jig!" cried Caitlin.

"We both get our dresses!" squealed Kaylee. Suddenly, the day had rebounded and was back in the Absolutely Terrific Zone.

That had been almost two hours earlier. Now, they sat around the pool laughing, enjoying each other's company. Evil Brittany Hall had gone down in flames. Kaylee and Caitlin were getting their solo dresses. All her best friends were having a great time. And she had just opened Caitlin's present to her—a t-shirt from the musical production of *Isle of Green Fire*, autographed by its star, Elena McGinty. Could the day get any better?

At that moment, the glass door at the far end of the pool room opened and a slim woman in tan cotton pants and a casual jacket with flowing red hair walked briskly toward their table, narrowly avoiding being splashed by the revelers in the pool along the way.

Kaylee could hardly believe her eyes. The day *had* gotten even better. Now it was absolutely complete.

The woman reached the table and gathered Kaylee O'Shay in a great hug. "Happy birthday my special munchkin!"

Kaylee hugged her back. "Thanks, Aunt Kat."

Aunt Kat now hugged her sister, who introduced her to Mrs. Hubbard. "Kat's quite an accomplished artist," Mrs. O'Shay explained proudly. "Owns a studio here in Chicago."

"Owned," Kat corrected her. "Recently sold it. I'm in transition, you might say. Moving to the Milwaukee area."

Every time Kaylee convinced herself that the day could not get any better, it somehow managed to. Aunt Kat living near Milwaukee? That was where Kaylee lived. She could not have felt luckier if she had bought a winning lottery ticket.

Suddenly, Aunt Kat turned to her niece and handed her an envelope. "Aren't you going to open my present?"

Kaylee smiled shyly and hugged her Aunt again. "Just having you here is great."

"Well, I'm hoping that you think what's in the envelope is great, too."

Now Kaylee was curious. She could not imagine anything that might be found in an envelope that could compete with having her favorite aunt at her best birthday party ever.

When she opened the card, however, she discovered once again that she had been wrong about virtually everything that had happened.

The card contained tickets. For the whole family. Plane tickets.

Kaylee could not speak. Her mouth hung open, her eyes bulging.

Aunt Kat was taking the O'Shay family to Ireland!

# Three

"I don't know if I can last until March!" was a frequent cry of exasperation heard from Kaylee as June sizzled into July. Just after the Trean Gaoth St. Patrick's Day shows—in eight long months—the O'Shays and Aunt Kat would board a plane for New York where they would then board another plane that would take them to the Emerald Isle. "Why can't we go sooner?"

Mrs. O'Shay typically rolled her eyes as she offered the explanation to her daughter for the umpteenth time. "When your Aunt Kat told me what she wanted to do, I thought it would be best if we did it during vacation time rather than missing school. So she scheduled it over spring break. That'll work out nicely for your father, too, since he works as a custodian at the school and is off at the same time."

Kaylee informed her mother that, in her opinion, it would work out even more nicely if she missed two weeks of boring classes and then returned from Ireland just in time for spring break.

"Just make sure you let your aunt know how much you appreciate this trip," said Mrs. O'Shay as the two cleared dishes after the evening meal. "I told her to save her money. But she wouldn't hear of it. Always been sort of a free sprit. Does what she wants."

Kaylee thought for a moment. "So are you and Kat opposites, Mom?"

"Hm?"

"You know," continued Kaylee, "she's the free spirit, you're the grounded one? Growing up, I'll bet she always did what she wanted, and you were probably the responsible one."

Her mother's eyes seemed to travel back in time for a moment. "I think we were both pretty strong-willed. We both knew what we wanted and went after it. Kat was just a little better at making the right choices."

"I resent that!" said Kaylee's father, Tom O'Shay, who had just wandered into the kitchen to catch the last part of this conversation. However, it was clear from his amused expression that his feelings were had not really been bruised. "I think you made an absolutely brilliant choice of husbands." He gave his wife a kiss on the cheek.

"But," said Mrs. O'Shay, "Kat has been a little better at making money."

"Which has always amazed me. I can't believe anyone can make a living off of art. Especially that modern stuff." Coffee cup now in hand, Mr. O'Shay retreated to the living room.

Kaylee returned her attention to her mother. "What bad choices did *you* make?"

It took Mrs. O'Shay a moment to recall the appropriate strand of conversation. When she did, she simply responded with a good-natured, "None of your business." Then her eyes popped wide and she glanced toward the living room. "But I certainly wasn't talking about your father. As choices go, he was . . . above average."

"I heard that!" said her father from the living room.

Kaylee's next Feis would be in mid-July, and so her summer slowed to a crawl. Without school, her responsibilities included a small number of household chores and two dance practices a week at Trean Gaoth Academy in Paavo. Consequently, when her Aunt Kat asked for help unpacking at her new apartment, Kaylee eagerly said yes. On a Monday morning, Kaylee hopped on her bicycle holding an address scribbled onto a scrap of paper and a vague idea of how to get there.

Aunt Kat's condo in Chicago had been in a newer development overlooking Lake Michigan. On those occasions when Kaylee had visited, she was awed by the breathtaking view. The condo had been beautifully furnished and the rooms had been enormous. One served as an office for her aunt. An indoor pool and an exercise room two floors below had made it a fun place to visit.

So Kaylee was a bit surprised when she hopped off her bicycle at the address given to her by her mother. Aunt Kat's new apartment was located just three blocks away from Rosemary's downtown business district, hardly a ten-minute walk from the Stitchin' Kitchen, which was the store Kaylee's mother owned. Aunt Kat's Chicago condo had been on the fourteenth floor. The building in Rosemary had only two stories, and Aunt Kat lived on the ground floor. The older bungalow across the street and the sleepy antique shop next to it hardly compared with the exciting view from the balcony at Aunt Kat's previous residence.

She had not brought a lock for her bicycle, but after a glance around, decided it would probably be safe enough if she laid it on the ground near some bushes at the corner of the building.

"Thanks for coming, Munchkin!" said Aunt Kat cheerily as Kaylee stepped from the dreary hallway into the more brightly-lit living room of the apartment. Aunt Kat was dressed in purple sweat pants, a tie-dye t-shirt and her long, red hair was held back with a colorful bandanna.

Kaylee gave her a hug. "What do you want me to do?"

Aunt Kat looked around the room and then pointed to several boxes in a corner. "Why don't you start by unpacking the books and putting them on the shelf."

Kaylee nodded and advanced to the boxes.

"Water?" asked Aunt Kat from behind.

Kaylee turned and accepted the bottle that Aunt Kat offered with a thank-you. No soda pop took up space in Aunt Kat's refrigerator. Only water and herbal teas. And she ate foods like sprouts and cheese curds and soy nuts. Kaylee actually enjoyed experimenting with many of these new foods, which often tasted great. However, she wished once in awhile Aunt Kat would loosen up and keep some cola and chips around the house.

"I'll be in the bedroom cleaning," called Aunt Kat in retreat.

Her aunt owned a small library, Kaylee decided, and she easily filled both shelving units. The extra books she stacked next to the last shelf, and then she flattened the boxes. Some of the books were related to art, although most of the books suggested that her aunt had an addiction to mysteries.

As Kaylee finished, she took in the living room, again, comparing it to her aunt's previous dwelling. This living room was no bigger than the one in the O'Shay house, and about half the size of the one at Aunt Kat's Chicago place. The floors here were narrow maple boards, the finish completely worn away in some of the high-traffic areas. The details of the trim along the high windows seemed obscured by perhaps a dozen thick coats of paint. The walls were smooth plaster, something not quite tan and not quite green—and certainly not quite what *she* would have picked for the color of *her* walls. The most striking feature was a quadruple bank of windows along the south side that allowed brilliant sunlight to flood the room. Her aunt had already set up an easel here, next to which reposed a stool and a metal case containing art supplies.

Aunt Kat emerged briefly from the bedroom and directed Kaylee to unpack several crates of carefully wrapped paintings—all with *Kat Newton* in the corner. Kaylee marveled at how her aunt seemed able to paint realistic landscapes that allowed one to almost feel the breeze and smell the cut grass, and then effortlessly create wild, surreal works that defied description. When Kaylee had leaned the last of the paintings against the living room wall, the duo broke for lunch. The sandwich was delicious, although at home, Kaylee was more accustomed to having spaghetti rings than sprouts, mushrooms, cucumbers and tomato with sour cream on whole wheat.

Aunt Kat asked about the previous school year and, of course, about dance.

"Sorry I couldn't make it in time to see you dance at the feis on Saturday," said Aunt Kat. "Finishing up at the gallery has been time consuming."

Kaylee could think of no delicate way to ask the question. Based on the age and tiny size of this apartment, Aunt Kat had obviously been forced to downsize. The poor woman was probably penniless, despite what Tom O'Shay believed. "Is your art gallery closing?"

Aunt Kat smiled and took a sip from her tea mug. "Oh, no, I sold it to an investor from New York. He paid a pretty good price for it, I might add."

All right, so it seemed that Aunt Kat had not gone broke. Just the opposite. But that did not explain why she had chosen to move from an incredible place in Chicago to the dingy little shoebox in Rosemary.

"So are you going to open an art store in Rosemary?" guessed Kaylee.

Aunt Kat's friendly eyes seemed to ponder this for a moment. "I'll bet a gallery would be a hit here. But if I do, it would not be for awhile. Couple of years, at least."

So she had not come to Rosemary because she was penniless or to open a new gallery. Kaylee wanted to come right out and ask, "Then why did you move from a fourteenth-floor view of Lake Michigan to . . . a view of Aunt Victoria's Antiques!" However, she thought such a question might be considered rude. And since no one had volunteered this information, she considered that maybe the reason was something that she was not supposed to know. She decided instead to satisfy another strand of her curiosity.

"Aunt Kat, what do you think Ireland will be like?"

Aunt Kat smiled across the table. "Munchkin, it's going to be gorgeous. Almost as gorgeous as you!"

If anyone else would have said such a thing, Kaylee would have blushed. "But what will we see?"

Aunt Kat thought for a moment. "I've never been there. But I've always wanted to go. I've heard it's lush and green most of the year. There's sheep and quaint shops and colorful country pubs and wonderful music. You can visit castles or bike the quiet countryside. The scenery is gorgeous. And the people are proud and friendly."

Kaylee nodded. "I've always wanted to go, too. At least since I started dancing. I was hoping that someday I'd qualify for the world championships and get to dance there."

Her aunt looked at Kaylee for a moment as if seeing something hidden suddenly emerge, something she had expected, yet something that still surprised her. "I know that you'll do it, Kaylee. And when that day comes, maybe you'll be more confident and relaxed because you'll have been to Ireland once already."

Kaylee smiled in admiration at her aunt and suddenly realized just how much she resembled Kaylee's mother, although Mrs. O'Shay wore her hair short.

"Aunt Kat, you're older than mom, right?"

Her aunt snorted ruefully. "By only two years."

"I was just wondering," continued Kaylee, "why you never went to Ireland before."

Aunt Kat wrinkled her nose. "Tim and I had talked about it." Kaylee recalled her Uncle Tim vaguely, but she and Kat had divorced when Kaylee was only six. "But then I got busy with the gallery and Tim got busy with the ad agency. Pretty soon we had no time for each other, much less a trip to Ireland."

Kaylee nodded as if she understood, although at the age of thirteen, the cementing together of relationships was difficult enough to comprehend. The dissolution of them was almost unfathomable.

"I'm glad we're going now. Well, eight months from now. And I'm glad we're all going together."

Her aunt smiled again, this time a little sadly, Kaylee thought.

"Me, too, Munchkin."

"But," added Kaylee, "I don't think I'm going to be able to wait until March! It's all I think about, almost."

She left her aunt's apartment smiling at the idea of the two of them exploring a moss-covered castle ruin jutting out of the brilliant green Irish countryside. The smile evaporated, however, as she heard the cries of distress.

"Help! Stop! Come back here!"

Kaylee looked across the street in the direction of the commotion and was surprised to see a woman lying on the sidewalk just outside of Aunt Victoria's Antique Shop. A second woman stood a few feet away, as if she had been heading away, but had turned back at the sound of the cries. Kaylee retrieved her bicycle and rode a bit closer.

"Please help me!" cried the woman on the ground. "She's a thief!"

The standing woman seemed confused, embarrassed, unable to decide on her course of action. Kaylee cautiously pedaled closer to the duo. The woman on the sidewalk seemed to have hurt herself. Or had the other woman hurt her? Although she wanted to be a good citizen, both of these people were strangers to her.

"Can I help?"

The woman sprawled on the walk appeared to be about forty with hair piled high on her head and so blonde and stiff that it might have been a painting of hair. She wore dark stockings, a too-short skirt, a fashionable jacket top and enough makeup for two middle-aged women—especially around the eyes. She appeared to have tripped coming through the doorway, and a trickle of blood oozed from a small scrape on her chin and through a tear at the knee of one of the stockings.

"Thief!" pointed the woman on the sidewalk, her eyes full of misty fury.

The standing woman, who wore designer jeans and a short-sleeve pullover top with a small purse slung over a shoulder, seemed bewildered and mortified.

"I'm not a thief!" she said. "I just came in to browse!"

"Ow!" said the woman on the ground, grimacing. "Liar! I saw you take it! It was there one minute and then you walked past and it was gone!"

Kaylee parked her bike and walked half a step closer. She had intended to help the woman on the ground, but this had suddenly become more complicated. Was she going to have to make a citizen's arrest as well?

The woman on the ground—who Kaylee assumed was the owner of Aunt Victoria's antiques—struggled a bit, and Kaylee, throwing caution into orbit, now knelt to help her up onto an elbow. She was hit by an overwhelming wave of lilac perfume along with another aroma she could not quite place.

"What do you think she took?" Kaylee asked.

"I didn't take anything!" protested the standing woman.

The shop owner pointed, her hand shaking slightly. "My crystal punch bowl! It was very valuable! A hundred years old!"

A puzzled look stole onto Kaylee's face. She looked at the standing woman who held her hands out wide. "Where would I hide a crystal punch bowl?"

"I don't know where you're hiding it," said the shop owner as Kaylee helped her, with some difficulty, the remaining way to her feet. "But it was a hundred years old!"

The standing woman rolled her eyes. "She's drunk!" Then she waved dismissively at the shop owner, whirled on a heel and marched resolutely away.

"I'm calling the police!" yelled the shop owner, but she received only a half-wave from the retreating customer, who ducked hastily into a red mini-van parked at the curb. Then the blonde woman turned and seemed to see Kaylee for the first time. When she spoke, the powerful wave of perfume-and-something-else hit Kaylee again. "What do you want?"

It took Kaylee a couple of tries to get the words started. "You looked like you needed help."

The shop owner straightened herself to the best of her current ability. "I can take care of myself." She turned towards the doorway and, after an unsteady step, twisted back. "She took my one hundred-year-old punch bowl! Did you see it?"

Again, Kaylee floundered for words. "I didn't see anything."

Now the woman looked down, fascinated by something else, as if she had now forgotten the punch bowl completely. "I've got a hole in my stocking! How did I do that?"

Kaylee wondered whether anything she said would make a difference. "I think you did it when you fell in the doorway. Do you need help getting cleaned up?"

The woman now turned fully around and squinted ruefully in Kaylee's direction. "I don't allow children in my shop unless they are accompanied by their parents. They make noise and break things."

"But you're hurt," pressed Kaylee.

The woman ignored her, opening the door of the shop. "I have to find that punch bowl." Then, in a hyper-dignified slow-motion, she disappeared inside the store.

Kaylee returned to her bicycle and was on her way in a moment. As she pedaled, she wondered what Aunt Kat had gotten herself into. She had traded a high-rise condo in Chicago for Aunt Victoria.

She hoped that all of Aunt Kat's new neighbors were not like that.

# *Four*

"I can try."

That was what Grandma Birdsall had said when Kaylee approached her about making a solo dress.

Try?

Kaylee could not understand it. Her grandmother was always sewing things. She had made quilts, purses, even the dress Kaylee had worn to the seventh-grade dance. And, of course, Grandma Birdsall had created the beautiful Trean Gaoth school dress, an amazing feat.

So what did she mean when she said she would "try" to make Kaylee's solo dress?

"Your grandmother needs more rest now," said Bethany O'Shay to her impatient daughter. "Unfortunately, her heart has not improved the way we had hoped. And when the doctors change her medication, there are often side-effects. Sometimes the result is that she's pretty wiped-out."

On one hand, Kaylee understood completely. She loved her grandmother. She wanted what was best for her. She knew that Grandma Birdsall always tried to please her granddaughter.

On the other hand, Kaylee was thirteen.

"I'll work as fast as I can," her grandmother promised.

"Green!" said Kaylee. "That's the color I've always wanted!"

They picked up several samples at the Stitchin' Kitchen.

Kaylee examined the tiny scraps on the car ride home. "Why can't we buy all the material now?"

"The dress design and the material have to be approved by Annie, the head of your dance school," her mother explained as she drove.

At Trean Gaoth Academy on Thursday night, Annie gave the green light to both.

"You're fortunate to have such a talented grandmother," Annie said. Grandma Birdsall, who had come along to observe, absolutely beamed.

*I just wish she were a faster grandmother,* thought Kaylee.

"You're lucky," said Caitlin. "My mom's already brought in three different designs. Annie says none of them is right for me. She's bringing number four at the end of practice today!"

A few days later, Mrs. O'Shay ordered the fabric from a supplier in Ireland, and Grandma Birdsall began the task of cutting out pattern pieces for the world's most beautiful and perfect solo dress.

"So how many days will it take?" asked Kaylee.

"For the fabric to arrive?" asked her grandmother.

"Until I can *wear* it!" cried Kaylee.

Grandma Birdsall bit her lip.

"Weeks?" asked Kaylee apprehensively.

"Your grandmother will work as fast as she can," Bethany O'Shay promised her daughter.

Kaylee sighed. For awhile, at least, her perfect solo dress and her trip to Ireland would remain at an impossibly distant point in the future.

On July 4th, Aunt Kat drove Kaylee and Will to Paavo for the big fireworks show at the college. In order to avoid walking for miles to the athletic fields from which the rockets would be launched, they arrived an hour early and were able to park close. The three spread out a blanket on the ground and munched on a granola mix Aunt Kat had brought.

"What a traffic jam!" said Will, gazing back at the long line of cars inching toward the parking lots a quarter mile behind them.

Aunt Kat looked and then smiled. "That's nothing compared to Chicago! And not just on holidays!"

Will tore his eyes away from the car carnage after a moment and regarded his aunt. "Do you like it here? As well as Chicago?"

"I like it better. In Chicago, I needed much longer arms to do this." Aunt Kat gave him a squeeze.

Only a thin ribbon of cerulean showed along the western horizon. They sat enjoying the cool night breeze and the background chatter of the thousands on blankets and lawn chairs. *It's almost like the camping area at a feis*, thought Kaylee.

"Would you two like to come to my apartment tomorrow morning?" asked Aunt Kat. "I've still got things to unpack. And I was thinking of doing a little painting. Walls, not canvas."

Will explained that he had a soccer camp that would last most of the day. Whenever Will mentioned soccer, Kaylee found herself feeling a little jealous. Ever since she had stopped playing two years ago, it seemed like her father spent more time with Will than with her. He rarely came to a feis, although he attended every one of Will's soccer games.

"Your father has always had a passion for soccer," her mother had explained.  "It's like your passion for dance."

Still, Kaylee wished her father would try a little harder. Thinking of fathers, she turned to Aunt Kat.

"What was Grandpa Joey like?"

The question seemed to take Aunt Kat by surprise. Grandpa Joey was Grandma Birdsall's first husband.  He had died when Kaylee was only a few days old.  Her second husband, Grandpa Birdsall, had passed away when Kaylee was five.

"My father?" Aunt Kat finally said.  "He was— funny.  A very kind man, but he had quite a sense of humor.  When my prom date came to get me, there was dad, sitting on the front porch with a shotgun across his lap."  She laughed at this memory, though both Will and Kaylee were horrified.

"Did he treat you and my mom the same?" asked Kaylee.

Aunt Kat shrugged.  "I guess so.  I never really thought about it.  He gave us both hugs.  Made us both do our homework and eat our vegetables."

Kaylee looked into the starry sky.  "What about sports?  Did you do any in school?  Did he come to see you?"

Aunt Kat thought for a moment and then opened her purse.  She produced a leather case and from this she pulled a small photograph, which she handed to her niece, along with a tiny keychain flashlight.  "I can't believe I never showed this to you before." The photo showed a much younger Aunt Kat, smiling broadly, wearing a track uniform. Her arm was around the neck of a freckled girl with a vast mop of curly hair.

A medal hung from younger Aunt Kat's neck.

"My dad took this picture," she said softly. "It was the day I won the conference title in the 800-meter run."

Kaylee squinted into the small circle of light. "Is the girl next to you your best friend?"

Aunt Kat smiled. "I guess you could say that. It's your mom!"

Now Kaylee looked more closely. "Wow! She was pretty back in the day."

Aunt Kat nodded. "Some people say you look a lot like her."

The darkness hid Kaylee's blush. "What event did my mom run?"

"Oh, your mom didn't run track," said Aunt Kat.

Kaylee had figured as much. Her mother had never seemed very interested in sports. Had never seemed particularly coordinated or physically strong. Aunt Kat was the athlete of the family, and her mother—it was now confirmed—had been a couch potato. And yet, Kaylee knew the two sisters had much in common. Her mother had admitted as much when she described both of them as strong-willed individuals who went after their dreams. One of Aunt Kat's dreams hung around the neck of the woman in the photo. But what about her mother? Kaylee knew Bethany O'Shay was fulfilling a dream by operating the Stitchin' Kitchen. But what about when she was a teenager? What had her dreams been then?

Kaylee was about to ask Aunt Kat that question when the fireworks began with a loud blast and a flash of color across the sky. The photo went away and the three settled back on the blanket to enjoy the show.

The colorful explosions in the night sky mesmerized Kaylee for a long while, but eventually she noticed things happening around her on the ground, too. Occasionally a couple would stroll past, hand-in-hand. Someone would pass with a carton of popcorn or a soft drink purchased from one of the kiosks that had sprung up at various spots along the sidewalks. In addition, electric service vehicles the size of golf carts glided noiselessly past every so often. One stopped not far from Kaylee's blanket at one point, and a man in dark green coveralls with the word MAINTENANCE on the back hopped off near a wire trash barrel. As he bent to pull the full garbage bag from the wire receptacle, a blue and gold aerial blast illuminated the area and Kaylee caught a glimpse of the man's face.

*He almost looks like Brittany's dad.*

Of course, that was a silly notion. Brittany Hall's father worked in a bank or something, not collecting garbage. Despite her certainty, Kaylee watched as the man hoisted the bag, tied it off and began to walk back toward the electric cart.

Another explosion lit up the grounds as if a flare had been ignited. This time, Kaylee had a full view of the man's face.

*That's got to be Mr. Hall,* Kaylee thought. Light brown hair, moustache, wide face. She had seen him many times at feiseanna and, before that, at soccer games. *But that wouldn't make any sense.*

She was about to pass it off as a remarkably close resemblance when the man looked up, locking eyes with Kaylee for just a moment. He looked away almost instantly, but in that half-second, Kaylee detected something. *He recognized me!* Then the cart moved silently off toward another wire trash container half a football field away. The fireworks continued to beckon from above, but Kaylee found herself distracted.

The maintenance worker was Mr. Hall. She was sure of it.

She was equally sure that Mr. Hall worked elsewhere. In fact, she had heard her dad mention it when she and Brittany had played on the same soccer team. And people who worked the night shift in maintenance did not buy their daughters beautiful new solo dance dresses that cost as much as Caribbean cruises. Or live in Oakton Heights, one of the most exclusive neighborhoods in the area, which was where Brittany lived.

*Maybe he got fired from his bank job,* Kaylee thought, remembering how her own father had lost his job at Rosemary Hardware. On the other hand, that would not have totally explained things, either. News like that would have spread through the middle school rumor network— even during the summer months—like wildfire, and would have spread even faster considering that popularity is a kind of gasoline where this sort of fire is concerned.

"Daydreaming?"

Aunt Kat smiled down at her niece and ran her fingers through Kaylee's hair. Kaylee smiled back and looked toward the sky, quickly forgetting everything except the beauty of the fireworks and the joy of savoring them with someone special.

The following morning, Kaylee biked to her aunt's and was hit in the face by an old t-shirt when she stepped inside the apartment.

"Slip that on. It's extra-large."

Kaylee gave her aunt the are-you-insane? look. "I'll drown in this!"

"It's to protect your clothes from paint," explained Aunt Kat. "It can go over what you're wearing."

They spent the next two hours rolling some color called "tope" onto the living room walls. Kaylee would have suggested a more dramatic hue, like bright green, if she had been asked. They broke for lunch and Aunt Kat constructed another delicious veggie sandwich for her niece, although Kaylee noticed that her aunt did not eat much herself.

"Stomach's a little off today," she explained. "In fact, I'll probably lie down for awhile after lunch. You did good work, Munchkin. Try again tomorrow?"

Kaylee nodded enthusiastically.

She left the apartment a few minutes later, planning to stop at Jackie's house on the way home. However, when she arrived at the bush where she normally stowed her bicycle, she discovered that it was missing. As she swung around toward the street, her heart skipped. A shaggy-haired boy who looked to be about fifteen or sixteen, wearing baggy pants and a black, sleeveless t-shirt, was sitting on the seat of her bike near the curb, both feet on the ground for support as he lit a cigarette.

"Hey!" cried Kaylee and ran toward her bike.

The boy glanced over his shoulder toward her, pushed off and, leaving behind a small cloud of smoke, began pedaling down the street. Fortunately, Kaylee had the advantage of a running start and grabbed the handlebar before he was able to reach full speed.

"This is my bike!"

The boy gave her the dead-eyes look, expelling jets of smoke, the cigarette bouncing madly as he spoke. "Better back off." There was a frightening quality in the coldness and deliberateness with which he muttered the words. For the first time it occurred to her that something bad could happen. Still, this was *her* bike. Her dad had bought it for her at a rummage sale, had fixed it up, had painted it—even adding white stripes. She could not simply let go and watch this foul creature ride off with it.

"But it's mine! You can't steal it!"

Now the dead eyes grew dark, and fear swelled inside of Kaylee. Still, her grip on the handlebar remained tight. If only her aunt would step outside of the apartment building and see what was happening. Or perhaps a police car would cruise past. But there was no police cruiser, and the apartment house door remained closed.

And so it surprised Kaylee when a voice rose above the booming of her heart.

"Hey, Nick! She's cool. Give her the bike."

The boy's features softened almost imperceptibly, and after another moment, he swung his leg over the seat and left Kaylee holding the bicycle.

Kaylee turned to face her rescuer, who strolled across the street. She could hardly believe her eyes.

It was Brittany Hall.

# *Five*

Kaylee felt torn. Brittany Hall was generally the last person she wanted to see. Yet, in this case, her rival seemed to be able to exert some kind of influence over the creepy boy-thief, who had now gotten off of her bicycle. Without a word, he smiled provocatively at Brittany and then turned and headed down the street on foot.

"You know him?" asked Kaylee incredulously, turning her attention to Brittany.

"Nick's okay," said Brittany. "Sometimes we hang out."

Kaylee had thought that Michael Black was the only boy Brittany ever hung out with, but she was really not surprised that her classmate at Kennedy Park Middle School would attract the interest of other adolescent males. Brittany had seemed to mature a bit more quickly than most of the girls her age. Kaylee had told herself that Brittany was simply oozing baby fat when the boys began to notice her curves as early as age ten. Now at thirteen, it was clear that there was more than baby fat to her nemesis. With her long blonde hair and piercing blue eyes, Brittany could have been a model. Today, with Brittany dressed in shorts and a lime green tank top, Kaylee understood Nick's smile.

The silence between them grew for a few moments before Kaylee spoke. "Thanks for the help."

Brittany shrugged. "Don't worry about it, O'Shrimp. I was just dragging the trash out to the curb when I saw you getting in Nick's face. I didn't want to see him have a meltdown. He's got some anger management issues."

Kaylee glanced across the street toward Aunt Victoria's Antiques. "Do you work there?"

Brittany followed her gaze and then spoke as if she were referencing a hospital infectious diseases ward. "Sort of. I dust the junk and sweep the floors a couple times a week. It's all overpriced garbage."

Kaylee thought about the awful woman who owned the shop, who had been so intoxicated that she had fallen onto the sidewalk and had accused a woman of taking something she could not possibly have taken. Working for a boss like that would be absolutely wretched. For the first time that she could remember, she felt a twinge of sympathy for Brittany Hall.

"At least it's a job," said Kaylee, not knowing what else to say. As far as Kaylee could recall, this was the first time that she and Brittany had ever had a conversation about something other than Kaylee's innate inferiority in every aspect of her existence.

But Kaylee knew this respite from Brittany's cruelty was temporary—like the time Brittany had picked Kaylee to be on her softball team in gym class. Kaylee had allowed herself to believe that Brittany had finally come to respect Kaylee's athletic ability. As it turned out, Brittany had simply chosen Kaylee to set her up for an embarrassing and painful collision with Heather Chandler, who had been chosen by the other team. Brittany's moments of civil discourse with her seemed mere rest stops on her trans-continental odyssey of intimidation, pain and self-aggrandizement.

Which is why Kaylee was completely unprepared for what Brittany said next.

"Sorry about the shoes."

Kaylee, who had been set to mutter a goodbye and push off down the street, now looked up at Brittany as if she had reported that the sky was not only falling, but also made of vanilla pudding.

"Your ghillies," added Brittany, seeing Kaylee's shocked look and mistaking it for confusion.

Earning her solo dress and having a great birthday party had helped take the edge off the hurt that Kaylee normally would have felt over missing two dances. Nonetheless, a part of her remained angry about the incident.

When Kaylee still said nothing, Brittany continued. "It was Heather. I forgot my ghillies in the car. I told Heather to see if she could borrow a pair from someone. I just meant for her to find another girl from Golden who was about my size and ask her if I could use her ghillies. But when Heather saw where you were camped, she just grabbed yours. She thought it would be funny."

Kaylee felt her lower lip jut out slightly. "It wasn't."

Brittany smiled without much enthusiasm. "Well, Heather's never been the brightest candle on the cake. But I never would have messed with another dancer's stuff without her permission. Not during a competition, anyway. She didn't tell me where she got them from until after."

Kaylee felt herself relax slightly. But then the memory of how Heather and Brittany had hidden her school dress during the middle school talent show rushed in. "You messed with my dress."

Brittany uttered a defensive laugh. "Yeah. Maybe that was a little too much."

Kaylee could feel her face warming. "A little?"

"But," Brittany said quickly, "Heather didn't wreck it. We knew you'd find it. Eventually. And I wouldn't have done it at a feis. A talent show is different. It's almost an invitation to prank someone! But dancing at a feis? If you're an Irish dancer, you know not to mess with that, how important it is."

Kaylee felt herself cooling by degrees. Apparently where Irish dance was concerned, there was some code of honor, some line in the sand that Brittany recognized as inviolable and which she would not cross. "Well, I still won my hornpipe. Got my solo dress." She did not know why it mattered to her that Brittany knew this.

"Nice," said Brittany, and Kaylee felt another icy barrier inside of her begin to soften. For the first time that Kaylee could recall, Brittany had responded kindly to one of her accomplishments. "Well, I gotta get back before my mom sticks her head out the front door and starts yelling."

"Is your mom shopping for antiques?" asked Kaylee.

Brittany laughed. "My mom owns the stupid store! Otherwise you'd never catch me in there in a million years!"

Then she was gone across the street.

As she rode toward Jackie's house, Kaylee found herself trying to imagine what it must be like for Brittany to work for the woman she had seen shouting wild accusations.

What it must be like to live with her.

To have her for a mom.

She could scarcely begin to process it, and instead she attempted to understand why Brittany had apologized. This seemed less daunting. Kaylee ultimately decided that it was because Brittany understood how much Irish dance meant to Kaylee. And the reason she understood this was probably because it meant just as much to Brittany.

# Six

Since the trip to Ireland was still an impossibly long period of time away, Kaylee began her assault on the second most incredible thing in her life: her unfinished solo dress.

"I wish Grandma would get it done," said Kaylee as she swept the floor one morning at the Stitchin' Kitchen, her mother's combination fabric shop and coffee bar.

Bethany O'Shay looked up from the labels she was preparing. "The special fabric hasn't come in yet. When it does, your grandmother will get started. It's just going to take time."

"She hasn't started?" Kaylee pouted as she swept without paying much attention, fanning the dust pile out of existence. "Grandma Birdsall said it might take months!"

Mrs. O'Shay looked at her daughter warily. "Well, we could always see if there's anything we can afford off the used dresses rack at the next feis."

Kaylee stopped sweeping and looked at her mother as if she were from another planet. "But Grandma finished my school dress so quickly! And she had heart troubles back then, too!" It still amazed Kaylee that her grandmother had sewn her school dress—a thing that is *never* done because school dresses must be identical and perfect. But Grandma Birdsall had pulled off an exact replica which had amazed Miss Annie, the owner of Kaylee's dance school. "If you would have come to me and asked if your grandmother could sew the dress, I would have said absolutely not," Annie had told them while examining her grandmother's handiwork. "We order them special. But this is . . . incredible!"

Mrs. O'Shay looked at her daughter sympathetically. "We've been over this before. Your grandmother's heart is not as strong as it was a few years ago."

This talk always horrified Kaylee. Three years ago, her grandmother had ended up in the hospital because of her heart. If it was even weaker now . . .

"And," continued Mrs. O'Shay, "you know how tired the new medicine makes her."

Kaylee had heard this a hundred times it seemed, and so she said nothing. However, she was surprised to see when she glanced down that she could not find her little dust pile.

At dance class on Thursday night, Miss Helen approached Kaylee and Caitlin as they were lacing on their ghillies.

"So. Here are my two who have now earned their solo dresses."

Both girls smiled. Kaylee felt glad to be hearing praise from Miss Helen, who usually seemed to hate her guts. Miss Helen was the oldest of the three teachers at Trean Gaoth—Kaylee guessed about sixty—and always seemed to wear the same dingy black sweats that smelled of cigarette smoke. She was as large as a vending machine and her unruly, mousy-gray hair was eternally mussed.

But Helen Cole had once been an Irish dance superstar. Every time Kaylee looked at Miss Helen, it seemed impossible to believe she had finished second in the world. Yet, Kaylee had seen the plaque at Golden Academy's hall of fame.

And so Miss Helen knew what it took to be successful. Unfortunately, she seemed to have serious doubts as to whether Kaylee possessed the right stuff.

Miss Helen looked at Caitlin as if considering which dessert to order off the menu. "I think red for you. That would be a good solo dress color. You will look marvelous!"

Caitlin smiled up at her. "That's sort of what my mom and I were thinking."

Then she turned her attention to Kaylee and frowned. She always seemed to be frowning when she looked at Kaylee. "Something light. Perhaps white or a pale blue."

Kaylee could not hold it back. "I was thinking green. Like an emerald. Annie already approved the design."

Miss Helen shook her head. "We already have several girls with deep-green dresses." Then she uttered a mirthless laugh. "And with the reddish sheen of your hair and your freckles, you would look like a Christmas tree!"

Miss Helen called over Annie and stood Kaylee like a condemned prisoner awaiting the firing squad. Miss Helen talked, Annie's brow furrowed, and then she nodded reluctantly. After she returned to her office, Miss Helen stepped forward, towering over Kaylee.

"Blue. It will be beautiful. Annie will talk to your grandmother."

And so it was done.  There would be no green dress.  Dance instructors usually offered guidance in selecting solo dresses, and that guidance was typically followed.

The two-hour practice that followed included stretching, drills, practicing their dance steps, and running through routines that Trean Gaoth Academy would perform at Milwaukee's lakefront Irish festival in late summer.  At the end of the session, Caitlin and Kaylee were both exhausted.  As they sat sipping at their water bottles from the edge of the dance floor, Miss Helen visited them once again.

"A good practice, tonight!  You girls are moving up quickly.  It would not surprise me if you are both in Open Prizewinner in all your dances before too long."

Kaylee felt her pulse quicken.  Open level competition?  That was only one level below PC, which Brittany Hall competed in!

"Of course, you must continue to work hard.  And no more of this silly soccer, eh?"

She glanced sideways at Kaylee as she said this.  Kaylee nodded glumly, recalling how passionately Miss Helen hated soccer.

In her first year of dance, Kaylee had skipped the school's big St. Patrick's Day show in Madison in order to play in a soccer tournament.  Miss Helen had not been happy.

Then in her second year, Kaylee had broken her leg during an indoor soccer match and had missed months of dance training and competition.  Miss Helen had seriously questioned Kaylee's commitment.

But the biggest reason Miss Helen hated soccer was because of Lizzie Martin.

Like everyone else who had danced for Trean Gaoth Academy for longer than a month or two, Caitlin understood the history behind Miss Helen's remarks. "You'd think that after eighteen years, Miss Helen would have gotten over that Lizzie chick," she said in a whisper after Miss Helen had moved on to talk to other panting dancers.

From what Kaylee understood, Miss Helen had been Lizzie Martin's dance instructor at Golden Academy and had poured herself into training the talented young woman. As a result, Lizzie had developed into one of the best dancers in the world, but then had suddenly quit. Also a talented soccer player, she had opted for that instead. Miss Helen had been devastated, and now, anyone who put soccer in front of Irish dance got an earful.

And there was something else—something that connected Kaylee herself to Miss Helen and to Lizzie Martin.

A letter.

Kaylee had never told Caitlin about it. Suddenly, this seemed to be something her friend needed to know.

"Ask your mom if you can sleep over tonight!" Kaylee blurted. When Mrs. Hubbard arrived, Caitlin quickly won approval, and when Tom O'Shay showed up, it was no great problem for Kaylee to twist him around her finger until he also said yes. They quickly stopped at the Hubbard residence to pick up overnight supplies for Caitlin, and then they headed to Rosemary.

After supper, the two girls retreated to Kaylee's room where Kaylee barricaded the door and retrieved the letter from a secret place.

"When my mom was thinking of closing the Stitchin' Kitchen, she had me cleaning out some boxes of junk in her office," Kaylee explained. "I found this. It was written to my mom back when she was in college."

She handed the letter to Caitlin who read it wide-eyed.

Hey,

Thanks for inviting me for pizza with you and the gang, but I can't on Friday. Big soccer game. What can I say? It's my life! We'll do the pizza some other time!

Lizzie Martin

"No way!" gasped Caitlin.

"Way!" countered Kaylee.

Caitlin stared at the letter for a moment. "Your mom and Lizzie Martin were friends! Did you tell your mom about finding it?"

Kaylee nodded. "She wasn't mad. I think she and Lizzie Martin must have had a fight or something a long time ago, because she didn't say much. She just seemed sort of sad."

Caitlin considered this revelation for a bit. "Does anyone else know about the letter?"

"Just my dad. But I think Miss Helen knows that my mom and Lizzie were friends. I think that's another reason that Miss Helen hates my guts."

Caitlin shrugged. "She didn't seem to hate your guts today. She actually seemed kind of proud of you."

"You'll notice she still got that dig about soccer in there," Kaylee reminded her. "And she talked Annie into changing the color of my solo dress!"

But her friend, Kaylee decided, was right. Miss Helen had seemed a bit warmer, more nurturing.

And Brittany Hall had apologized.

She wondered whether these were simply coincidences, or whether when one turns thirteen, the world turns topsy-turvy—and there's not much anyone can do about it.

# Seven

The music seemed to flow around and through her simultaneously as Kaylee moved gracefully across the stage, her arms pinned to her sides, her toes pointed and precise. When she finally reached the end of her dance and bowed to the judge and musician, she knew that she had nailed her reel.

Aunt Kat flashed Kaylee a thumbs-up from the spectator area. Of course, Kaylee could not respond, since she had to stand at attention along the back of the stage until all the dancers in her group had finished.

Afterwards, she, Aunt Kat and Mrs. O'Shay made their way back to where the family had thrown down blankets and erected camp chairs. Kaylee always loved dancing at feiseanna, but having her Aunt Kat here to see this one made it even better.

"You were wonderful, athletic, beautiful," said Aunt Kat, smiling and giving her niece a hug. "Of course, that doesn't surprise me at all. You are your mother's child."

Kaylee almost laughed when she saw her mother's horrified look. Wonderful and beautiful? Maybe. But her mother had never been an athlete.

"What a colorful, vibrant place," Aunt Kat continued. "I can see why you're in love with Irish dance!" Then she drew an old sketch book out of the satchel leaning against her camp stool. Aunt Kat had been drawing in the book all morning on and off.

The Milwaukee Summerfeis was held at an attractive, suburban college which allowed all eight dance stages to fit inside the fieldhouse. The fieldhouse also provided plenty of room for dancers to camp, and so only the vendors occupied the outer hallway. The only thing missing from the feis was Caitlin, who had flown to Tennessee with her family for a week-long vacation.

"I can't believe you're going to miss Summerfeis!" Kaylee had said indignantly at their most recent dance practice.

"My mom found a feis in Nashville that same weekend!" Caitlin had responded. "So I'll still be dancing. We just won't be together."

Kaylee flitted over to the stage where Jordi and Hannah were dancing. They were a year younger, so Kaylee had never competed against them. She also watched April Lee—who competed in the Advanced Beginner level. "But it's not the same as when Caitlin's here," she complained to her mother. "She's like my shadow!"

Hard shoes were danced last at the Milwaukee Summerfeis, and with her soft shoe dances complete, Kaylee slipped out of her dress and pulled on jam pants and a t-shirt. Then, after begging money from her mother, she set off to find food.

But first, she could not resist a side trip to the results area.

A long strip of yellow caution tape had been strung about six feet from the wall in the wide hallway outside the fieldhouse.  Posters attached to the wall indicated the dance level and age group.  Kaylee found her category and frowned.  Neither her reel nor her slip jig had been posted.

"Why can't they just tell you how you did right at the stage after you dance?" she muttered to herself.

"'Cause the judges are chicken," said a familiar voice.

Brittany Hall stood beside her, also checking the results.  "I'm looking to see how a friend did.  I don't dance until later.  But at least I remembered my shoes today!"

Another first: Kaylee smiled in response to something Brittany had said.  Kaylee noticed that today Brittany wore a tight-fitting, pink t-shirt and dark green shorts with the word GOLDEN printed across the backside.

"I'm hoping to get top five today in PC," Brittany continued airily.  "If I do, my dad said he'd get me a new cell phone!"

*Preliminary Champion!*  That was the second-highest competition category in all of Irish dance!  Kaylee had frequently fantasized that someday, she would compete on the same stage against Brittany—and beat her!  But it looked like Brittany would always be a step ahead.

At *least* one step.

"I'm hoping to be qualified for Open Prizewinner in all my dances by the end of the day," Kaylee blurted.

"Oh yeah?" said Brittany, cocking an eyebrow.  "How close are you?"

"Pretty close," said Kaylee evasively.

Brittany seemed to be sizing her up. "I thought you just earned your solo dress."

"Oh I've had it for awhile!" said Kaylee, a bit too eagerly. "I mean . . . I don't have the actual dress. I'm qualified, but we haven't picked out a dress yet. We're looking for just the right one."

Brittany grabbed her elbow. "Come on! I'll show you a really cool one!"

In a few moments, they stood in front of one of the garment vendors. A white-haired man smiled kindly at them and then turned back to the customers directly in front of him. Several brand-new Irish dance dresses hung from a display bracket next to his tables, and Brittany plucked one off the rack.

"Isn't this awesome?"

In fact, it was the most completely awesome thing that Kaylee had ever seen.

"It's light blue!"

"Duh!" responded Brittany.

"That's the color my dance teacher thinks I should wear."

Not only was it a brilliant, iridescent blue, it was resplendent with silver and cobalt and red highlights that sparkled as if a jewelry store had exploded.

Brittany held it up to Kaylee. "It looks about your size. Too small for me or I'd have my dad buy it."

Kaylee imagined herself in the dress on stage, dancing her hornpipe. Dancing in Open competition.

Then she spotted the price tag.

Suddenly she was back in her school dress, wondering whether she would be a Novice for another month, a year or the rest of her life. Although she was not positive, she thought that the price of the dress was similar to what her father had mentioned when he talked about how much he had paid for his most recent car.

"I'll show it to my mother later," said Kaylee, smiling thinly, helping Brittany replace it on the rack. As she did so, she checked the prices of two other dresses, but noticed that there was not much difference. As Kaylee took one last look at the dress, she remembered the white solo dress that she had seen Brittany wear. "Where did you get your white dress?"

Brittany buzzed her lips dismissively. "That was my *old* dress. We bought it in Chicago. This year, I got a new one. All the way from Ireland!"

Kaylee imagined that Brittany's new Irish dress would make the price tag on the beautiful blue dress seem puny by comparison. Suddenly, Kaylee did not feel like spending her mother's money on expensive hot pretzels or pizza slices.

"I guess I better check to see whether it's time to do my hard shoes."

"I'm on stage seven," said Brittany. "Come on over later and you can see my dress."

That's just what Kaylee wanted to see: Brittany in a beautiful dress, the likes of which Kaylee could never afford.

"Great!"

Back at Camp O'Shay, Kaylee dug a PB&J sandwich out of the mini-cooler.

"No nachos or hot dog?" asked Mrs. O'Shay.

She handed her mother the money. "Solo dresses are expensive."

Kaylee felt completely unprepared for the look of sympathy that flooded her mother's eyes, followed by an enormous hug. Then she looked around the camp area. "Where's Aunt Kat?"

Mrs. O'Shay appeared anxious as she answered. "Kat wasn't feeling well. Decided to call it an early day."

"But," pouted Kaylee, "she didn't see my hard shoes! Those are my best dances!"

Mrs. O'Shay nodded glumly. "She'll see them next time." Then she glanced at her watch. "And speaking of time, you'd better get back into your dress. Your hornpipe should be coming up before too long."

She danced her hornpipe and then, half an hour later, her treble jig. However, Kaylee did not feel particularly enthusiastic. Caitlin was dancing in Tennessee, her Aunt Kat had gone home and she could not in a million years afford the beautiful blue dress in just the color that Miss Helen had suggested. Her anxious imagination began to wonder whether her two arch-enemies, Miss Helen and Brittany, had somehow conspired together to make her feel this way. That would explain their recent, uncharacteristic kindness toward her.

Miss Helen: *Get a blue dress, Kaylee!*

Brittany: *Here's a blue dress . . . but you can never afford it!*

Get her comfortable, set her up, and then—bam! What a sweet plan.

As she exited the stage following her treble jig, she nearly ran over a boy dancer.

"Excuse me," she muttered, but when she looked up, she saw that it was Riley, a thirteen-year-old who danced for Golden Academy.

A very cute thirteen-year-old.

"Oh! Are you up next on this stage?"

Riley flashed a brilliant, gorgeous smile that almost melted Kaylee and confirmed more than ever that he was very nearly the equal of Michael Black. "I'm on stage six. I came over to see you dance."

Kaylee's mind whirled. When a boy came to see you dance . . . that was a good thing, right?

"Thanks!" Kaylee followed him to a spot behind the spectators. Then she turned, looked back at the stage and let her eyes fall to the floor. "I don't think I did very well. I wasn't really into it today. I was hoping to qualify for Open in all my dances, but now . . . I don't know."

Riley nodded. "I know it's tougher for girls because there are so many in each competition."

Kaylee had once been told that girls outnumbered boys in Irish dance by a ratio of about forty to one. In some competitions, there might be only two or three boys in an age category while there might be fifty or more girls.

"But," Riley continued, "it still took me a long time to work my way up to PC."

"How long does it take most people to go from Novice to Open Prizewinner in all of their dances?" Kaylee wondered aloud.

Riley was ready with an answer. "I heard Clarissa tell some of the girls at Golden that hardly anyone gets first place in all their dances right away." Clarissa Golden was the owner of Golden Academy. "She said you might get one here and there, and it can take months. Even years. She said to be patient."

Years? Kaylee could not even imagine such a thing. After getting a gold medal in her hornpipe at the previous feis, she was now hungry for more.

But she was now also more afraid than ever to check the results posters. What if she placed poorly? Or what if she failed to place in any of her dances?

They wove their way through the crowd and into the wide lobby area outside the fieldhouse.

"Clarissa always tells us whether we get a first place or a fifth place doesn't really matter," continued Riley as they emerged into this slightly quieter area of the feis. "She says any place shows that you're getting noticed by the judges, and that's a good thing."

This news surprised Kaylee, who had always harbored the impression that Golden Academy dancers were drilled relentlessly to accept nothing other than gold. Riley made Clarissa Golden sound almost like . . .

Like Annie.

"I looked for you at the feis in Chicago last month," Kaylee heard herself say, and then she blushed, realizing how it might sound.

"Clarissa wanted us to rest up for Nationals, which was over the Fourth of July weekend," Riley said matter-of-factly.

Kaylee's mouth fell open. "You danced at Nationals?"

"It was fun," said Riley, "It was incredible. Very intimidating. I didn't make re-calls."

Kaylee remembered Miss Helen explaining once that re-calling occurred in the higher-level dances. It meant that the judges had ranked a dancer among the best in the competition. He or she was then usually called back on stage later to receive an award, but whether it was first place or fortieth, no one knew until the final announcements were made.

"Just getting to Nationals is . . ." Somehow, Kaylee always had trouble coming up with words that did not make her sound like a low-grade moron when she was around Riley. ". . . Good! Cool! Really cool!"

*Great*, thought Kaylee. *Queen of the one-syllable word! If I'm ever transported into prehistoric times, I'll be able to communicate really well with the cave men!*

"Well," said Riley, "I'd better get over to stage two. How do I look?" He stretched out his arms theatrically.

*Don't sound like an idiot*, she told herself. *All those vocabulary units in seventh grade! I ought to be able to remember something!*

"Winsome!" Kaylee blurted.

*Oh, that was brilliant! Go back to cave talk!*

Riley did not seem to notice. As they walked, he asked her how she had been spending her summer, what she was looking forward to in eighth grade, and before she knew it, she was *answering* and not even thinking about which words she was using.

On their way to Riley's stage, they passed stage seven. That's where Brittany said she would be competing, Kaylee remembered. She paused for a moment and squinted through the crowd to where two girls were dancing the treble jig. Both had dark hair. After a completing their steps, they bowed and moved off to make way for the next two, and that was when Kaylee spotted Brittany. And Brittany's new dress.

It was green, the exact color Kaylee had been thinking of when she had first talked to Miss Helen. Silver and purple glittering accents peppered it, forming intricate Celtic knots. Her dream dress moved across the stage beautifully, athletically.

And    it    belonged    to    Brittany    Hall.

# *Eight*

Aunt Kat looked tired when Kaylee biked to her apartment the day after the Milwaukee Summerfeis.

"I can come back tomorrow or Tuesday," she told her aunt.

Aunt Kat would have none of it. "It's a nice day. No sense for me to be sitting around inside just because I'm not quite up to climbing Mt. Everest." And so they had walked to Rosemary's downtown, where Aunt Kat had bought her a cone at the ice cream shop.

"Aren't you going to have any?" asked Kaylee as the two faced each other in one of the antique-style booths.

"Stomach's not quite right today," said Kat, twisting her face to illustrate the point. "Next time I'll eat a whole quart! With chocolate sauce!"

As Kaylee worked on the cookie dough cone, Kat raised her glass of water as in a toast. "Here's to the fine day you had at yesterday's feis!"

Kaylee wrinkled her nose. "It was okay. But I need more first places. That's the only way I can move up to Open in everything!"

"But you got a first in your reel! And a third in your hornpipe! I'm sorry I wasn't there to see your hard shoe dances."

Kaylee had gotten a first in her hornpipe in Chicago, so now she was qualified for Open Prizewinner in two of her four required dances. She could have danced her hornpipe in the Open category in Milwaukee, except that the deadline for changing from Novice to the Open division had already passed for that feis.

"Maybe you can come to St. Louis with us in August!" said Kaylee excitedly. "With you there, I'm sure I could get first place in my treble jig and slip jig!"

Aunt Kat laughed. "You're pretty confident! You realize, don't you, that all those other girls are hoping to win, too!"

"But I've got something they don't."

"I know," said Kat, nodding. "Your mother tells me you're always practicing. Wearing holes in your bedroom carpet, the way I hear it."

"That's not it," said Kaylee. "They don't have *you* cheering them on!"

Aunt Kat reached across the table and gave her niece an enormous hug.

By the time they walked back to the apartment, Aunt Kat was done for.

"Guess I should pace myself until I'm feeling one hundred percent," she said wearily. "Or at least ninety. I'm a pretty pathetic specimen for a thirty-seven-year-old woman."

"I think you're beautiful, Aunt Kat," said Kaylee as she hugged her goodbye. But as Aunt Kat waved her niece out the door, it seemed to Kaylee that she looked much older than thirty-seven.

Caitlin had returned from Tennessee in a grumpy mood. "The best place I got was a third," she fumed as they warmed up for practice on Thursday evening. She had tried gamely to smile when Kaylee told Caitlin about her first place in the reel. But the update on her solo dress seemed to infuriate Caitlin the most. "My mother told me my solo dress might take six months to get here! Or more!"

The Hubbards had ordered Caitlin's dress from a shop in Ireland. Kaylee decided not to tell her friend what Mrs. O'Shay had said: "They *say* the dress will take six months, but I've heard of some who wait more than a year!" That sort of news would have driven Caitlin over the edge.

"I thought my grandmother would be able to make my dress," said Kaylee sympathetically. "But she's been so tired lately that mom says we may have to buy a used one."

"Wonderful," said Caitlin dourly. "You'll have your solo dress before me. You'll be doing all your dances in Open Prizewinner before me. I'll probably still be in Novice while I'm watching you at the World Championships."

Kaylee laughed, but then she saw that her friend was not joining in. "Are you okay?"

"I'm just great!" said Caitlin the way a person says it when she means quite the opposite.

"I thought you'd be happy about going to Tennessee, about my first place . . ."

Caitlin said nothing, and then Tara, who was in her twenties and the youngest of the three Trean Gaoth instructors, began the practice. Caitlin's mood did not improve at all during their workout, and she changed her shoes and disappeared quickly once it had ended.

Kaylee's mother waved from the parked car as her daughter approached.    Mrs. O'Shay rarely came in to watch the workouts, preferring to sit in her car with a book or to run errands in Paavo.

"We're going to have a late supper at Aunt Kat's," she reminded her daughter.    Your father and Will are meeting us."

They arrived in about twenty minutes and Kaylee dug into the soup and sandwiches that her mother had brought.    Will, who seemed to eat twice the amount that a skinny twelve-year-old should require, downed three sandwiches almost—it seemed to Kaylee—without chewing.    She noticed that Aunt Kat ate mostly soup.

"I hope you're feeling better than last weekend, Aunt Kat," said Kaylee as Will's ability to annihilate the food diminished.

Kaylee noticed the sisters exchanging an anxious glance, and then Aunt Kat plunged ahead, addressing both Kaylee and Will.    "That's partly why we're all having dinner together tonight.    I think it's important that your mother and I treat you as young adults.    And I want to be honest and up-front with you about what's going on."

*What's going on?*    Kaylee had not suspected that anything was going on.    However, she did not like the direction this seemed to be taking.    When adults offered to let children in on secrets, it was never anything good.

"I've been sick for longer than just the past week," continued Aunt Kat.    "But lately, I've had to get different treatments and take new medicines that really knock me out.    It would have been almost impossible for me to run the gallery while receiving the treatments, and that's why I sold it.    I moved here to be near all of you in case I needed help while I'm getting through this."

Kaylee listed as if in a trance, and she could tell from the look on Will's face that he was responding to Aunt Kat's explanation in the same way. *This can't be true,* thought Kaylee. Aunt Kat can't be seriously sick. She's always been so careful about what she eats, and she was a champion athlete and she walks everywhere . . .

Aunt Kat turned toward Kaylee and smiled. "That's why I had to leave the feis early on Saturday. And why I felt so tired after our little walk." Then she moved her eyes to Will. "And it's why I couldn't come to your soccer game on Tuesday."

"But," interrupted Kaylee, "you're going to get better soon, right?"

Now Aunt Kat smiled so radiantly that she looked not only completely healthy, but ten years younger. "I plan to, sweetheart. I'm a fighter. I see what I want, and I go after it! And you'd better believe I want to beat this!"

Now Will spoke up. "But what's making you sick?"

Aunt Kat's smile faded somewhat, but when she spoke, her inner strength was irrefutable. "I have cancer." Both children gasped, and tears welled in the corners of their eyes. "Now don't cry! Millions of people get this disease, and many of them beat it! You don't think I'm going to just sit around and give up, do you?"

Both children shook their heads, although they appeared ready to burst into tears again at a moment's notice.

"That's why I'm taking treatments at a special hospital in Milwaukee," Aunt Kat said confidently. "The doctors are very confident that I'll respond to the therapy. I may not have as much energy as you'd like all of the time, though."

With shaking voices, both Kaylee and Will promised that this would not matter. They would help in any way they could.

"And I may lose my hair," said Aunt Kat with a wink.

Two mouths dropped open.

"So you both understand?" asked Mrs. O'Shay, a slight tremble in her voice. "And you'll both help out when necessary? No questions asked?"

The two children nodded enthusiastically and then rushed around the table to hug their aunt—who Kaylee now noticed *did* seem somewhat thinner than she had remembered.

"And for heavens sake," said Kat, as if wrestling twin octopi, "don't get all teary over this! Together, we're going to win!"

But tears of gratitude ran down Aunt Kat's cheeks as she said this.

Normally, Kaylee and Will would have been forced to wash the dishes at such an occasion, but Aunt Kat had an automatic dishwasher, and on top of this, the adults apparently felt that the children needed a break in order to recover from the evening's trauma. In the small yard fronting Aunt Kat's apartment, Will kicked a soccer ball, while Kaylee wandered beneath the streetlamp near the curb, kicking stones and occasionally breaking into a dance step. She noticed that the lights were on inside Aunt Victoria's Antiques, although the sign in the front door said CLOSED.

The day had left her with a kind of numbness. First, Caitlin had hurt her with what seemed to be jealousy. *How could Caitlin, with all her money and talent,*

*ever be jealous of me?* she wondered.   Then Aunt Kat's news
had been like a refrigerator dropped onto her heart.
Maybe both of these awful occurrences were dreams—no,
nightmares—from which she would awake to a world
where her aunt was healthy and solo dresses were
delivered the week after you ordered them.

Almost without being conscious of it, Kaylee found
she had crossed the quiet street and now stood on the
sidewalk in front of Aunt Victoria's.  Like a cat to yarn, she
found herself drawn to the lit window, and inside, Brittany
swept the floor between rows of what she had described as
junk.   Kaylee's immediate reaction was to pull back from
the window, but Brittany looked up too quickly, leaned
the broom against a table filled with knick-knacks, and
came to the door.

"Out shopping for late night bargains, O'Shrimp?"
asked Brittany as she stepped out onto the sidewalk.

"Just saw the light," muttered Kaylee.

"I'm helping the old lady get everything ready for
her *Big Weekend*," said Brittany, with sarcastic emphasis on
the last two words.  "Big twenty percent off sale.  I'm sure
the police will have to be called in to direct traffic it'll be so
successful."

Kaylee thought of her own mother's shop.   "My
mom's business doesn't get a lot of customers, either."

"Neither does this dump," noted Brittany, poking a
hand toward the building behind her.   "But the stuff in
here is so overpriced, that whenever she sells something,
it's a big payday.   But I don't think I've ever seen more
than six people in the shop at the same time."

Suddenly, Kaylee felt more bold than she had ever
felt in Brittany's presence.   "Hey, can you not call me
O'Shrimp anymore?"

For an instant, Brittany looked as though she did not understand. Kaylee figured that, since she had done it for years, calling Kaylee "O'Shrimp" had simply seemed natural. Then her countenance softened. "Oh, sure. Kaylee!"

Kaylee smiled, suddenly wondering whether her request had sounded as silly as the nickname itself. "Well, I better get back to my aunt's."

"Yeah," said Brittany. "She stopped in at the shop yesterday. Saw me rearranging the dust and asked if I knew you. Boy, is she skinny."

Part of Kaylee wanted to tell Brittany about her aunt's cancer, although another part felt that this would violate some intimate family trust. *Why do I care what Brittany thinks?* "She's been sick," said Kaylee finally.

Brittany nodded, almost as if she really understood. "I figured."

So Brittany had noticed that her aunt looked ill. Kaylee wondered whether she herself was the only one who had not seemed to see the signs. Or maybe she had noticed, but had denied the obvious.

A sudden voice from the shop door cut through the quiet night air. "Brittany! Are you ready to go home?"

Mrs. Hall appeared in the doorway. Although her eyes still betrayed a rheumy glassiness, she did not seem as disoriented or combative as when Kaylee had seen her previously.

"Who are you talking to?"

Brittany turned with the requisite eye roll. "Just someone from school, ma."

Mrs. Hall squinted in Kaylee's direction but offered no greeting. With her heavy makeup and her hair piled atop her head the way it was, Mrs. Hall looked much older than Kaylee's own mother. Straightening herself as if she were meeting foreign royalty, she began a slow glide toward the curb where the largest, whitest, boxiest-looking sport-utility vehicle Kaylee had ever seen rested like the cornerstone of the Great Pyramid of Giza. "Come," she called without turning back. "The cats need feeding."

Brittany smiled weakly. "We've got six cats. They eat so much, we may as well have a horse!"

Kaylee returned the smile. "That's sort of what it's like having a brother."

Brittany took a step toward the SUV into which her mother had already disappeared, then faced Kaylee again and spoke with a lowered voice. "Hey! You want to come to a party on Saturday?"

This was definitely some sort of dream. Brittany, inviting her to a party?

"It's at my house! Nine!"

Kaylee took a step backward. "In the morning?"

Brittany rolled her eyes. "At night, clueless!"

Kaylee nodded as if she were invited to parties all the time. Then she turned and made her way back toward the boy juggling the soccer ball in the cool evening shadows.

# Nine

Kaylee slept later than usual on Friday. Normally, school days were the only time she wanted to sleep late. During summer vacation, there was so much to do that did not involve multiplication or adverbs or the Bill of Rights, and she could hardly wait to leap out of bed and dive into the wonders of the day.

Today, however, it was past ten o'clock before she dragged herself to the kitchen. Her grandmother sat in one of the chairs, her nose pressed close to the morning newspaper spread out in front of her. For a change, Grandma Birdsall appeared alert and refreshed.

"Well, it's good to see you up and about, little Miss Sunshine," said Grandma Birdsall cheerily.

Kaylee grunted and proceeded to the cereal cabinet. *I feel like Little Miss Zombie,* she thought. After preparing her cereal, she sat across the table from her grandmother. Kaylee munched spoonfuls and then, assessing her grandmother's current level of energy and remembering her solo dress, asked her Grandma Birdsall how the project was coming.

Grandma Birdsall looked up from the newspaper and rubbed the backs of her hands. "I wish I were younger. There was a day when I could have finished the dress in a week or two! But as you know, I can only work for little bits now."

"Is it going to be done soon?" Kaylee asked a bit too restlessly.

"It's going to be awhile, Kaylee.    The new blue material just arrived, you know."

Kaylee could see in her grandmother's face how acutely she felt the burden of her granddaughter's disappointment. Kaylee also knew what she should do: be gracious. Her grandmother was trying her hardest. She wanted to please Kaylee so badly. Kaylee should have said something like, *Don't worry, Grandma. I know you'll get it done eventually. And if I have to wait a little, that'll just make it so much better the first time I wear it!*

But that was not what came out.

"I don't know why I tried so hard to get first place if I still have to wear a school dress!"

Then she pushed away from the table and headed back to her room—where she felt even more horrible than she had upon crawling out of bed. Kaylee stayed there for half an hour, and when she emerged, she found the kitchen empty. The cereal bowl that she had left behind at the table had been emptied and rinsed and now sat in the sink. Her grandmother's bedroom door stood closed.

Then she spotted a note on the counter. Her mother had left it, asking Kaylee to bike to the Stitchin' Kitchen after lunch to help with some cleaning. *And P.S., pick up your room!*

Kaylee groaned. Fridays were supposed to be fun days. This one had gotten off to a terrible start. She decided that a call to Caitlin might be just the thing to make her feel better. Unfortunately, Caitlin's mood had not changed since the previous night.

"I don't see why you're being such a grouch!" Kaylee told her friend. "You're getting an expensive dress from Ireland!"

"Oh, right, and money solves every problem, doesn't it?" countered Caitlin—before hanging up the phone.

Kaylee stomped back to her room, slammed her door, buried her face in a pillow and screamed. Then the tears came, but they were not born of sadness. These tears burned with anger—anger at her family for not being able to buy her a proper dress, at her grandmother for being so slow, at her best friend for being unreasonable and at herself for being . . . thirteen!

But mostly, Kaylee felt angry that her Aunt Kat was sick. It was so unfair! Her aunt was the kindest most wonderful and creative person she had ever known. She exercised and ate all the right foods. Cancer was for people who smoked or ate red meat three meals a day or drank gallons of preservative-laced soft drinks. Aunt Kat did none of those things!

Kaylee hammered her mattress with her fists.

Aunt Kat had told her she was going to beat this. But Kaylee knew that lots of people with cancer did not beat it.

She rolled onto her back and pulled the pillow over her face, crying "It's not fair!" into it at the top of her lungs, muffling the sound so no one else could hear. And she realized that she was not simply angry. She was scared.

Reaching to the floor, she grabbed the first loose object she could find, which was a jogging shoe. She threw it savagely, bouncing it off a wall and onto the top of her bureau, which was cluttered with medals and dance memorabilia. Something clattered to the floor.

Kaylee stood, wiped a hot tear off her cheek and retrieved the object from the foot of the bureau. She held a trophy in her hand, a trophy with a marble base, a tiny blue column and a gold, heart-shaped plastic arch from which a medal hung. The medal had been her first in Irish dance, and despite its extravagant cost, her father had bought the little trophy from an engraver at the feis in order to display this first triumph.

The fall had broken the gold, plastic arch, which Kaylee now held in her hand. She set the pieces back atop her dresser and collapsed again onto her bed. She knew that this should make her cry, for Irish dance meant the world to her.

However, today she felt nothing.

# Ten

On Saturday morning, Kaylee biked to Jackie's. She found her friend in tears.

"Angelo Zizzo is hurt!" she cried, sitting on her bed, an Angelo Zizzo poster spread out on the comforter in front of her. A barren spot on the Angelo Zizzo Shrine Wall showed where Jackie had removed the poster. "His knee! He might be out for months!"

Kaylee tried to work up some sympathy for her friend, but Angelo Zizzo was half a world away and had not the slightest inkling that either Kaylee or Jackie existed.

"Sorry," said Kaylee. "Want to do something tonight?"

Jackie sniffed, raised her head. "I was thinking a candlelight vigil. We could face Italy. Chant 'We love you, Angelo'!"

"I was thinking maybe a sleepover," said Kaylee.

Yeah," said Jackie heavily, "but I probably wouldn't sleep much. I'd be too upset."

"That's kind of the point of a sleepover," said Kaylee. "If you don't stay up all night, it's not a success."

"I suppose we could put in some DVDs of Angelo Zizzo in last year's championship game," said Jackie, brightening. "An all-night Angelo Zizzo marathon might be just the thing!"

Kaylee grimaced. "I was thinking we could watch some movies. Maybe funny ones. Wouldn't that make you feel better?"

Jackie leaned onto her side and shook her head. "I just don't think anything would seem very funny to me tonight."

Kaylee hesitated, and then blurted, "I got invited to a party tonight." She had not intended to tell Jackie. In fact, she had decided to simply forget about it. Just what business did she have attending a party thrown by Brittany Hall? That was for people who had attained the highest level of Popularity at Kennedy Park Middle School. Kaylee felt like she was still in the basement. However, Jackie was being a pain. On a gorgeous summer day, she sat in her bedroom moaning about some overpaid professional athlete who might as well have lived in a different universe.

Jackie rolled onto her stomach, hardly paying attention. "Oh really? A party? Who's having it?"

Kaylee took a deep breath. "Brittany Hall."

Suddenly, Jackie sat bolt upright, the oddness of this situation chasing away—at least for a moment—even the need to grieve over Angelo Zizzo's injuries. "This is a joke, right?"

Kaylee shook her head.

"I take back what I said before," said Jackie, a smile creeping onto her face. "*This* is funny. You guys have been mortal enemies for, like, forever!"

Kaylee told her how Brittany had apologized about the shoes and how they had talked in front of her mother's antique shop twice.

Jackie pondered this development for some time. "You do realize that this could be a set-up. Remember the black eye in gym class?"

Kaylee remembered.

"If you're on her own turf, surrounded by all of her future-convict friends, it could be worse than anything that has ever happened to you in school or on the soccer field," warned Jackie. "Your body might never be found!"

Kaylee felt herself getting angry. "Isn't it possible that she just thinks I'm cool?"

Jackie laughed. "We are definitely not cool. The only place you see our names next to cool is in the dictionary of antonyms."

Kaylee suddenly found herself ready to hurl a million mean words at Jackie. *Maybe people would think you were cooler if you didn't mope around hugging a poster like an idiot.* She realized, however, it would probably be better if she simply left. As she headed for the bedroom door, Jackie asked, "Are you going? To her party?"

Kaylee shrugged and departed without a word.

As she biked home, Kaylee felt more lonely and upset than ever. All Caitlin seemed to care about was how long it would take for her dress to arrive from Ireland. Meanwhile, Jackie had dissolved into some fantasy world where Angelo Zizzo's life was inexorably linked to Rosemary, Wisconsin. Neither of her best friends seemed to care one bit about what Kaylee was going through.

She found her father in the garage changing the oil on the car. Her mother would still be at the Stitchin' Kitchen.

"Dad, can I sleep over at Jackie's tonight?"

Her father grunted as he tightened something underneath the vehicle. "Did you check to see if there's anything on the family calendar?"

Kaylee told him that she had, and it was all clear.

Tom O'Shay slid out from under the car and grabbed a funnel from the shelf. "No problem. What time do I need to drop you?"

"I can bike."

Her father nodded. "Have fun. I know you and Jackie always do."

At seven-thirty, Kaylee slipped on her backpack and headed out the door. "Have a good time, sweetheart. Call when you get there!"

Kaylee nodded and rushed out before she would have to give too many details about her evening. She biked to downtown Rosemary and parked on the sidewalk in front of the Stitchin' Kitchen. From her pocket she pulled the spare key and quickly let herself in. After that, she pulled the bicycle inside and shut the door.

This business represented her mother's dream. Bethany O'Shay had been an elementary school teacher when Kaylee was younger, but about four years ago, she had decided to open her own shop. "Lots of women like to sew," she had explained to the family. "And they like good coffee, too. Here they can have both." She had rented space in a former antique shop in downtown Rosemary, a place with large display windows out front and a worn hardwood floor. A charming coffee bar nestled near the front windows, surrounded by half a dozen sewing stations on which people might rent time. On these same machines, Mrs. O'Shay also taught lessons throughout the day. Her clients sewed and sipped happily.

The dimness of dusk stole across the street outside. A light in back of the store burned each night so that the police could see inside as they rolled past on patrol, and so Kaylee had no trouble finding her way to her mother's office. Once there, she sat at her mother's old wooden desk and waited for another ten minutes. Then she picked up the telephone and dialed her home number.

"Hello?"

"Hi, Mom! I made it fine!" Sweat broke out on her palms. Was there a slight tremor in her voice? If her mother asked to speak to Mrs. Kizobu, her plan was dead.

"All right, honey. Say hi to the Kizobus for us. Love you!"

She hung up the phone with a relieved sigh. Now all she had to do was . . . wait. Brittany had said nine o-clock, and so she had an hour to waste. Nothing would be less cool than appearing over-eager and showing up as the first guest—as if she had nothing else to do on a Saturday night.

As Kaylee sat in the mostly-dark room, she remembered finding the Lizzie Martin letter here in a box of her mother's old college papers, a letter that connected her mother to the person Miss Helen hated most in the world. A letter that explained so much, yet which seemed to leave so many unanswered questions as well.

How close had her mother and Lizzie Martin really been? Had they been casual acquaintances, or were they best friends like Kaylee and Jackie? Had they simply grown apart over the years? Perhaps Lizzie Martin had moved across the country and her mother had not seen her since. When Kaylee had talked to her mother about the letter, she had gotten the impression that something bad had happened.

Maybe there had been a big fight. But over what? A guy, maybe? *Maybe over dad!* Kaylee laughed at this thought and tried to chase the absurdity out of her mind.

Or perhaps Lizzie Martin had died. That could also explain why Mrs. O'Shay seemed reluctant to talk about her.

She would someday ask her mother about all of these things. For now, however, she had resolved to never be like Lizzie Martin, to never betray what was really important in life.

A shiver ran through Kaylee, and she hugged herself.

On the day she had stumbled across the Lizzie Martin letter, it had almost seemed like she had been fated to find it—like a puzzle piece or the answer to part of a riddle. It shed light on a facet of her life that, until then, had seemed beyond explanation. Tonight, however, she felt like a trespasser in this room, as if her presence there were all wrong.

The night was warm, but she shivered again.

And she waited.

# Eleven

A few minutes after nine, Kaylee pulled her bicycle out the front of her mother's shop and locked the door behind her. Her backpack, which contained sleepover supplies, she left in her mother's office. It took only ten minutes to pedal through back streets to Oakton Heights, Brittany's neighborhood.

The homes in Oakton Heights, Kaylee noticed, were newer and larger than her own, even bigger and nicer than Caitlin's house in Paavo. Her father had once described it as a place where people could pretend to be a little better than everyone else, and a little better off than they actually were. Kaylee was not quite sure what he meant, but it had sounded like some sort of insult.

A narrow band of blue-gold clung to the western horizon as Kaylee zipped into the neighborhood, but the canopy of ancient oaks and maples made the night complete before she had gone very far. After another minute, she turned onto Killdeer Court and found herself in front of the white colonial-style home where Brittany lived. Faux pillars and black shutters accented the front of the two-story home, which was lit by blue-tinted decorative spotlights. Kaylee rested her bike on the lawn, but then thought better of it. This did not seem like the sort of home that would have bicycles abandoned in the yard. Instead, she pushed it to the side of the garage and leaned it against the outside wall. Then Kaylee climbed the front steps and rang the doorbell, whose chimes sounded like the grandfather clock at Jackie's house.

Brittany opened the door a few moments later, looking miffed. "Don't ring the bell!" she hissed. "You'll wake the old lady!"

Kaylee apologized and stepped inside.

The lighting in Brittany's house was subdued, but even so, Kaylee could make out cream-colored tile in the entryway, and the pillar theme seemed to have been continued indoors. Thick, plum-colored carpeting stretched out into a lacey-looking room on the left, and a shiny, dark dining room set surrounded by gold-framed wall paintings rested in a room on the right. Aside from an underlying pungent aroma that betrayed the presence of Brittany's six cats, everything seemed incredibly neat, and Kaylee made a move to take off her shoes.

"Don't," said Brittany. "We're out back around the fire pit."

They continued into the kitchen, where Kaylee found the first signs of disorder: bags of chips, cookies and a crumb-covered empty cardboard pizza circle. "Grab some food if you want," said Brittany, who Kaylee noticed was wearing a rainbow halter and very short shorts. Helped by the sort of makeup application Kaylee had never seen at Kennedy Park Middle School, Brittany could have easily passed for a twenty-year-old.

"Is your mom sick?" asked Kaylee as they approached the sliding glass door at the back of the kitchen.

Brittany half turned back toward her. "Hm?"

"You said she's asleep already?"

Brittany gave a rueful look toward the upstairs. "Yeah, she's asleep. A few vodka martinis will do that to you! After eight o'clock, I've got the house to myself almost every night."

Kaylee's shocked look made Brittany laugh. "What? Does your family belong to some weird cult that forbids alcohol?"

Kaylee shook her head. Her father had an occasional beer. Once in great awhile, her mother would open a wine cooler. However, she could not imagine either of them drinking to the point where they would pass out.

The sliding glass door opened in front of the two girls, and Nick, the brooding, unsuccessful bike-napper, slid through the gap, a lit cigarette dangling from his lips. He aimed a leer at Brittany and then gave a good-natured, glassy-eyed nod to Kaylee, which convinced her that he either did not remember or recognize her before disappearing behind a door across the kitchen.

"That's the bathroom," said Brittany, pointing after Nick.

They stepped out into the night onto a small white, wooden deck, and Kaylee immediately heard the sounds of voices raised in revelry a short distance away. She smelled smoke and saw the flicker of light that meant a fire behind some trees and ornamental bushes. Kaylee usually loved sitting around a campfire, however, she could not get into the party spirit. It was as if she could feel an adult presence hidden just out of sight, waiting for the right moment to thunder in and admonish Nick for the cigarettes and Brittany for her revealing outfit. As they made their way along a wide garden path, Kaylee could keep it in no longer. "Isn't your father going to be mad if he catches Nick smoking in the house?"

"Don't worry about my dad," said Brittany. "He's working late in Milwaukee at the bank. He'll stop at a restaurant after. As long as we're out of here by eleven, he won't know a thing."

"Working?" gasped Kaylee. "On a Saturday night?"

"They make him put in a lot of extra hours, but he gets paid a bundle for it," said Brittany. "That's how we can afford to live in this shack."

"So," said Kaylee, hardly able to comprehend the amount of unsupervised time Brittany enjoyed, "your dad is never home before eleven? That must be awful to never see him." As she said this, Kaylee was reminded that she sometimes felt that soccer took her father out of the picture almost as much.

"It's not every day," said Brittany as they walked. "He started working more last year. Right after my mom bought a new super-sized SUV."

Kaylee remembered the white monstrosity in front of the antique shop.

"And she remodeled the kitchen," continued Brittany. "Dad said she was spending money like it grew on trees. He even suggested that we move to a smaller place because he was having trouble making payments. But mom laid down the law, told him she'd get a lawyer and take everything he owned if he tried to make her do that. So he started working overtime at the bank."

The realization hit Kaylee suddenly. "So we're on our own!" She had never been to a party—or any sort of social event—where there had not been adult chaperones.

"Yeah," said Brittany. The light from the fire grew brighter all of a sudden. "Isn't it great?"

As they made a turn in the path, the fire came into view, set in a clearing inside a pit carefully ringed by decorative bricks. Lawn chairs and larger chunks of log were set haphazardly around the blaze and a dozen or so people sat or stood, animated by their conversation and the flicker of the flames.

As they approached the group, Brittany pointed to a red metal cooler sitting on the ground. "Help yourself to something to drink." Then she worked her way toward a group of boys standing off to the left.

Kaylee took a deep breath and looked around. She recognized only one other girl from her grade in school, and she was not a person with whom Kaylee normally associated.

She was one of the Cool People.

Most of the crowd seemed older by a couple of years. All seemed to be holding cans or bottles, but they were not filled with root beer or fruit punch.

*What does a person do at this kind of party?* Kaylee wondered. All of the parties she had previously attended had been to celebrate something. There had been games and cake and everything had been brightly lit.

A boy with soft, yellow hair came past Kaylee from the direction of the house. She saw he was carrying a guitar case and an amplifier. Behind him shuffled a girl unrolling a long electrical cord as she went. Kaylee recognized her as Heather Chandler. She smiled at Kaylee as she passed, but the smile dissolved into a menacing frown once she recognized the new arrival. In a few minutes, the yellow-haired boy—whose name, Kaylee gathered from shouts in his direction, was Chad—began singing a popular, melancholy song about love.

"Keep the amp turned low," Brittany cautioned him as he finished. "We don't want the neighbors to call the cops!"

The thought of police arriving sent a stab of fear and guilt through Kaylee. No way did she want her parents to ever find out about this party.

Chad continued to play low, background music, and Kaylee decided that he was pretty good. Maybe if she found something to drink and took a seat by the fire, she would eventually relax and start to have a good time.

Opening the cooler indicated by Brittany and digging through the ice chunks, she found several beer varieties in cans and bottles and even a couple of wine coolers. She dug deeper. Where was the pop?

"What you looking for?" said a short girl with a wide, flat face and thick lips. She leaned in quite close and Kaylee noticed her breath smelled like rotten fruit.

Kaylee mentioned that she could not find the soda pop.

"I'll set you up!" said the girl, who walked Kaylee unsteadily to a wooden bench set back from the fire. On this bench were some two-liter bottles of pop, some smaller glass bottles, as well as plastic cups. "Cola?" asked the girl thickly, and Kaylee nodded. The girl half-filled a plastic cup with cola from one of the two-liter bottles and then, before Kaylee could utter a protest, filled most of the remainder with liquid from one of the smaller glass bottles. "Enjoy!" said the girl with a wide smile, and then she flounced off to talk with a group of boys.

Kaylee took a sniff of the concoction. It smelled more like medicine than a soft drink. *I wonder how it'll taste?* Kaylee figured it must taste pretty good, or all of these kids would not want to risk breaking the law and getting caught by their parents just to drink it. On the other hand, Will had snuck a sip of their father's beer one time and told Kaylee that it tasted disgusting.

She found an empty seat by the fire and, holding her drink as if it were a ticking bomb, settled onto an upended slice of log. For a few minutes, she sat there as if made of granite. Then she noticed the stars. Directly above, the trees parted to allow a gorgeous view of the glittering heavens. Kaylee felt her shoulders relax. Chad's mellow music drifted through the night air. The campfire crackled hypnotically a few feet in front of her. She was at her first real teen party.

She felt pretty good.

Kaylee considered the cup cradled in both hands. *I guess I should start having a good time.*

She brought the cup up an inch before she spotted Heather Chandler standing just behind Brittany across the campfire. A wicked smile played on Heather's lips as she stared directly at Kaylee.

*She probably knows this is my first drink.* Kaylee did not want to give Heather the satisfaction of witnessing the milestone, and so she lowered the cup again to lap level.

A boy walked past close and paused as if to examine the fire. Looking up, Kaylee saw that it was Michael Black. Her heart thumped loudly in her chest, making her wonder whether he could hear it. Every girl at Kennedy Park Middle School would have traded places with her right now, she guessed. In the flickering light from the fire pit, he looked even more handsome and mysterious than ever.

*I may as well make conversation.*

"Hi!"

He looked over at her, but his face betrayed little emotion. "Hey," he said it a flat voice.

Kaylee felt awkward but pushed on. "Pretty cool party, hey?"

But Michael Black had begun walking away halfway through the question, and Kaylee felt her ears grow warm as he approached a small group near the cooler, a group that included his girlfriend, Brittany. He stood next to her, slipping his arm casually around her waist, his hand ending up in her back pocket.

*He didn't seem to know I even existed,* Kaylee told herself. Then she reconsidered. *He didn't seem to CARE that I existed!*

Kaylee suddenly wished that Riley were there. He had come looking for her at the feis. *He* cared.

She looked around at the others. They seemed to be talking and laughing and not simply sitting in front of the campfire as if waiting for the smores supplies to arrive. *Maybe I need to try harder to fit in. Maybe I'm the problem.*

She listened to the music for awhile and then raised the cup another inch—but was distracted this time by laughter on the far side of the campfire. The flat-faced girl had a can of beer in her hands and Brittany and several others were encouraging her to chug it.

"Come on, Rachel!" shouted a boy. "Don't be a wimp!"

Rachel drank, tilting her head farther and farther back. Some liquid escaped out the sides of her mouth, but then she held the empty can aloft, grinning, and tossed it into the fire. She seemed momentarily confused, but then someone handed her a cup.

"Again!" shouted Brittany, and Rachel began gulping down the dark liquid—which Kaylee suspected was similar to what was in her own cup. Half a dozen people clapped as the empty cup dropped to the ground.

"More!" shouted a stringy-haired boy in a tank top to Rachel's left, but Rachel's face now carried a pained expression and a hand crept to her stomach.

"My eight-year-old sister could do better than that!" shouted stringy-hair.

"Come on, Rachel!" taunted another boy. "We thought you were tougher than that!"

Rachel no longer seemed to hear what they were saying. A worried look had appeared on her face. Suddenly, she stumbled to the bushes behind her, dropped to her knees and threw up. Again and again.

Kaylee stood and took a step toward the girl to see if she needed help. However, she noticed that everyone else had turned away from the retching teen as if she never existed and had resumed their conversations around the campfire.

All except one.

Heather Chandler walked up behind Rachel, who was on all fours, panting like a sick puppy. *Maybe Heather's going to help her*, Kaylee thought. However, Heather shook her head, pulled out a cigarette from somewhere and lit it.

Kaylee could scarcely believe it. *Heather's one of Kennedy Park's best athletes! Why would she do something so stupid as smoke a cigarette? Didn't they hurt your lungs, slow you down?*

Then Heather leaned forward and blew a huge cloud of smoke onto the sick girl. "Rachel, you are the biggest loser I've ever seen!"

As Heather turned back toward the campfire, her eyes locked with Kaylee's. "Drink up, O'Shrimp! Maybe you can give Rachel some competition for that Biggest Loser title!"

Kaylee's heart began to thump hard. She raised the cup again. *Heather thinks I'm weak! But there's lots of things I can do that Heather can't!*

However, as she considered this, the only thing that came to mind was Irish dance. And for some reason, this made her think of Miss Helen. What would her teacher think, seeing her sitting here ready to take her first drink? Would she think, *No discipline,* and shake her head? *She doesn't have what it takes to be a great athlete. As I suspected, she's just like Lizzie Martin.*

Chad had taken a break from playing the guitar, and now Nick jumped in and took his seat. He turned the knob on the amp way up and began scratching out a raucous melody that Kaylee was certain would shake the leaves from the trees and possibly even kill them at their roots. Several people started clapping and making loud hooting sounds.

*What am I doing here?* thought Kaylee. She did not want to drink whatever Rachel had mixed in her cup. She did not want to force someone to do something embarrassing and then belittle them afterwards. She did not want to lie to her parents and let down the people she really cared for.

The drink fell to the ground and Kaylee headed back down the garden path. Everyone was cheering on Nick and did not seem to notice her departure. However, halfway to the house, she encountered the stringy-haired boy who had been urging Rachel to drink more.

"Hey!" he said, coming to a stop in front of her. "I'm Zack. You're Heather's friend, right?"

Zack smelled like cigarette smoke, and he clutched what Kaylee assumed, based on his thick speech, was probably not his first beer of the evening.

"I'm not Heather's friend," said Kaylee, trying to move around him. "I'm just . . . going."

Zach placed a hand on her shoulder. "What's your rush?" His eyes seemed to clear just slightly as they traveled over her from head to toe. "The party's just getting started!" He reached into his baggy pants pocket and pulled out an unopened can of beer, which he handed to Kaylee. Then, the pressure of his fingers increasing slightly on her shoulder, he began to shepherd her back in the direction of the screeching music.

Zach reached over to Kaylee's beer and popped the top, giving her a watery grin that served as an invitation to drink up. Kaylee did not know what to do. She did not want to simply drop the can and run away. That would forever cement her reputation as one of the least cool people in school. At least among Brittany's crowd.

*Why do I care what they think?* Kaylee asked herself, knowing all the while that an impossible to articulate reason existed.

She made an effort to slow their progress and then turned toward Zack. "Bathroom," she said, as if that should explain everything. Kaylee made a move toward the house, leaving Zack staring after her, when without warning, a girl she did not recognize with streaky blonde and cinnamon hair came sprinting toward her.

"Cops!" cried the girl in a frantic whisper. She raced past Kaylee, who followed to the campfire where

Nick's guitar music abruptly stopped, leaving the wooded clearing eerily quiet.

"There's a police cruiser in your driveway and a cop at the front door!" hissed the girl to Brittany. "I wouldn't have seen it except I went up to use the bathroom!"

Without a word, everyone took off running. Only Brittany headed toward the house, carrying the guitar and amp and collecting the extension cord as she went. The rest sprinted for the trees.

*What should I do?* Kaylee wondered, her mouth suddenly dry, the full can of beer finally slipping from her fingers. She had never run from the police before. She had never *needed* to run from the police before.

But she could not let them find her here. She thought of her parents, her aunt, Miss Helen.

And then she sprinted.

The woods seemed to be laced with several narrow trails, not the nicely-manicured, wood chip-covered kind that led from Brittany's house to the fire pit, but the sort made by children on the way to a hidden treehouse. Kaylee chose one and plunged into the darkness, not knowing where she would emerge. She ran for a few moments before she heard a girl's scream off to her left. Several seconds later, she heard a male voice curse loudly. What was happening?

Then someone cried, "Cops in the woods!"

Kaylee ran faster. Her breath tearing from her in frantic rasps. Neighbors must have reported the noise of Nick's guitar, Kaylee guessed. Several police officers probably had circled into the woods, figuring that the partying teens would make a run for it. If only she could find a way out of these trees, she prayed, she would never do anything this foolish again.

A hand closed on her forearm and Kaylee jerked to a halt.

"All right, you!" said a stern voice, and Kaylee realized immediately that it was over. She found herself in the grip of one of the policemen whose form rose in front of her vaguely in the dark. "Don't struggle now!"

Struggle? The thought had never entered Kaylee's mind to put up a struggle against a police officer. She had been taught that the police were there to help, like fire fighters and doctors and nurses. She would as likely have struggled against a lifeguard trying to pull her from shark-infested waters.

Police officers were there to stop the bad guys.

*It's over*, she thought, imagining the disgrace she would feel when they brought her home to her parents. Or would she have to go to jail? She had no idea. This was a part of the world she had never traveled—had never imagined she would travel.

Then a crashing sound like a wild animal trampling the underbrush grew louder and someone burst out of the heavy growth onto the path. The stringy hair and baggy clothes seemed to suggest that this was Zack, who seemed to have plunged wildly through the darkness, not caring whether he was on a trail. He struck the police officer with a shoulder, though the officer was solidly built so that Zack moved him only a few inches.

"That's enough now!" shouted the officer, momentarily losing his grip on Kaylee so as to steady this new and less cooperative arrival. Realizing that she was free, some instinct seemed to take over, and Kaylee raced back in the direction she had come. She would not physically struggle against a police officer, but that would not stop her from running.

She took the first side trail and kept going until the shouts seemed to be a fair distance behind her. The side trail ended suddenly at the backyard of a house three doors down the street from the Halls. Kaylee sat behind a tree where the forest met the neatly-mowed lawn and waited. She could see the police cruiser in Brittany's driveway from her vantage point. After what seemed forever, another car pulled in next to it and a man who Kaylee assumed was Mr. Hall got out, although the dim blue floodlights and distance made it impossible to tell.

More time passed, and Kaylee began to feel faintly chilled. The woods had been quiet for a long time. She wondered whether the police were waiting for her to come out of hiding. The thought was irrational. Even the officer who had grabbed her on the path could not possibly have gotten a good look at her face in the dark. Hardly anyone at the party had even known who she was. And while Brittany had many faults, Kaylee knew she would not rat out anyone. In short, no one—particularly the police—would ever know that Kaylee had attended Brittany's party.

Just as she had reconciled herself to a long walk home, she noticed activity again and the police cruiser backed down the driveway and disappeared into the night. Kaylee waited another ten minutes before carefully making her way back to the Hall's. As she passed Mr. Hall's car, Kaylee noticed that he had left the driver's side door hanging open in his haste to find out what was going on after discovering a police cruiser in his driveway. Kaylee turned toward the house, which appeared dark and lifeless now. She wondered whether Brittany was already asleep. Had she been grounded? Had her father roused Mrs. Hall, and had both of them teamed up to express their outrage at Brittany's behavior?

Or was Brittany's family life far too different for Kaylee to imagine?

Before collecting her bike, Kaylee decided she had better close Mr. Hall's car door so that the dome light would go off and not attract bugs. As she placed a hand on the open door, she recognized something on the front seat—a pair of dark green coveralls with the word MAINTENANCE on the back.

She shut the door as quietly as she could and then slipped around to the side of the garage. No one seemed to have noticed her bicycle leaned against the outside wall, and in a minute, she was speeding through the cool night air.

Kaylee struggled to understand what she had seen. Brittany had said her father was working late at the bank. However, it appeared to Kaylee that he was actually doing night maintenance for the college in Paavo. *Typical Brittany,* thought Kaylee. *Too proud to admit that her father works nights as a janitor.*

Too proud to admit that her father did the same type of work that Kaylee's father did.

But there was another possibility.

The thought struck her like electricity. Perhaps Brittany did not *know* her father worked nights as a maintenance man, his sacrifice to keep his wife and daughter in a nice house in Oakton Heights. Maybe *he* was the proud one, and that was why he had left the coveralls in the car rather than wearing them into the house. It certainly made more sense, now that Kaylee thought about it, than a banker working until eleven on a Saturday night.

Kaylee had always assumed that Brittany had everything. She was beginning to realize that people were far more of a mystery than she had previously thought.

Her first stop was the Stitchin' Kitchen where she retrieved her backpack. Minutes later, she stood on tiptoes, tapping on the glass of Jackie's bedroom window.

"Of course I'm not asleep," said Jackie when she unlocked the back door to let in her friend. "I told you I'd be in mourning all night!"

Kaylee could not help but hug her friend. "Mind if I spend the night? Even if you don't sleep at all?"

"Course not," said Jackie. "But I thought you were going to hang out with the *cool* kids tonight."

"That's right," said Kaylee. "It just took me awhile to get here!"

# *Twelve*

August proved to be full of surprises.

Caitlin provided the first surprise when she suddenly ceased being angry with Kaylee. One Thursday at dance practice, Caitlin's smile and chatter returned and the two girls carried on as if there had never been a rift between them.

Kaylee subsequently learned that Caitlin's good humor owed much to a new dress. Not the dress from Ireland, which Mrs. Hubbard estimated would arrive no earlier than the following April. Caitlin's parents had decided—prompted, Kaylee guessed, by their daughter's gloomy demeanor—that a "temporary" dress would be in order to bridge the gap between July and April. Or May. Or June or whenever the dress from Ireland finally arrived. ("I know a woman who says she's been waiting fifteen months for the dress she ordered," April's mother mentioned one evening after practice. This did not make Mrs. Hubbard feel one bit better.)

And so the Hubbards had gone dress shopping at the July feiseanna. At most competitions, an area was set aside where parents could hang dresses that they wished to sell, dresses that their own children had outgrown or grown weary of. Mrs. Hubbard had found a nearly-new angelic white dress with blue and silver glittering highlights. "When the Irish dress arrives, we can sell this one," Mrs. Hubbard had explained. Mr. Hubbard thought Caitlin looked so good in the white dress that perhaps they could simply cancel their order for the garment from Ireland—but neither Caitlin nor her mother would have anything to do with *that* idea.

Kaylee and her mother had looked at dresses, too, during the July feis. "Everything that looks nice is way too expensive," said Mrs. O'Shay. "And everything that isn't too expensive . . . well, it's *all* too expensive!"

So Kaylee had ridden to the August feis in St, Louis with Caitlin, Mrs. Hubbard, Aunt Kat and her own mother, resigned to the notion that she would have to wear her school dress once again—even though she had earned firsts in *two* different dances and was, in fact, *doubly* qualified to wear a solo dress.

If only her Grandma Birdsall could sew faster. Unfortunately, the last time she had checked on her grandmother's progress, so little had been accomplished that Kaylee had to hold back her tears.

Stupid heart condition.

Aunt Kat had brought her sketch book to St. Louis, as she had to the two feiseanna prior to it. As soon as the families spread blankets and unfolded their portable chairs at the back of the arena, Aunt Kat took off to search for inspiration.

"Your aunt is amazing!" Mrs. Hubbard said, looking after her. "Such energy! If not for the bandanna, you'd never suspect!"

Aunt Kat had started wearing explosively imaginative bandannas after her hair grew thin.

"That's a side-effect of the treatments," Aunt Kat explained. "I'll do just fine wearing a bandanna. In fact, I'm the sort of woman who was born to wear a brightly-colored bandanna!" She struck a fashion model pose and Kaylee could not help but laugh.

Kaylee felt constantly amazed at her aunt's upbeat attitude, her ability to smile in the face of this frightening challenge. However, Kaylee felt herself growing more optimistic, too. "We get to choose how we deal with challenges," her aunt told Kaylee. "You and I, Kaylee, we're a lot alike. We'll never choose to give up! We're like mountain climbers, always looking toward the top!"

Her aunt's marked improvement was August's second surprise. Aunt Kat reported that the treatments seemed to be going just as well as expected and that the doctors said she was a wonderful patient.

"And, when this is all over, my hair *will* grow back!"

As if to justify their sense of optimism, Aunt Kat's strength seemed to have returned in large measure. She was back to walking two miles a day and generally seemed to have as much energy as she had before her diagnosis.

At feiseanna, Aunt Kat was never without her sketchbook. The color and movement of the dancers held her under a kind of spell, providing her with an inspiration that other subjects did not.

"You've got quite a wait before either of you dance," Mrs. Hubbard reported.

As Caitlin pulled makeup containers from a satchel, Kaylee slipped on her wig and began the process of pinning it in place. As she was finishing, Aunt Kat rushed up out of breath. At first Kaylee thought her aunt was having some sort of relapse, but then Kat hurried them over to the dress marketplace and held up her find. It was a beautiful sky blue, exactly as Miss Helen had suggested, and the dress fit as if it had been made just for Kaylee. The sleeves revealed a few worn spots, but Mrs. O'Shay was confident that they would not show too much—or could be suitably repaired by Grandma Birdsall. The only problem was the price. "It's a few hundred more than we had anticipated spending," said Kaylee's mother.

"Oh, I think maybe I can help with that," Aunt Kat winked, and just like that, the dress—August's third surprise—was in Kaylee's arms.

"Can I wear it today?" asked Kaylee excitedly when they reached their camp.

Her mother smiled proudly. "I don't see why not. You've earned the right!"

Kaylee slipped on the new dress again as soon as her mother relinquished the hanger. Caitlin was just in the process of donning what they had dubbed her "angel dress".

Mrs. O'Shay took a step back from the girls, cocked her head and broke into an enormous smile. "Why look at you two!"

"I think I'm going to cry!" added Mrs. Hubbard.

The two girls would be competing against each other in only the treble jig. Kaylee had been moved into Open Prizewinner in the hornpipe and the reel, while Caitlin still danced at the Novice level in those. Caitlin, on the other hand, had moved up into the Open slip jig. Kaylee's slip jig, by her own admission, had "a long way to go".

"I'm glad we don't have to dance against each other very often," said Kaylee. "I'm always afraid one of us will place and the other won't."

"I don't mind," said Caitlin. "We may as well get used to it. Someday we'll have to dance against each other at the world championships, won't we?"

Kaylee had never looked at it that way. "I guess we both can't be world champion."

"Yeah," said Caitlin with a sigh and then a wicked grin. "Too bad for you."

Both girls laughed.

A short time later, the two friends and fourteen others lined the back of the stage as the treble jig music began. Kaylee found herself paired with a girl in a black and red school dress. As she stood ready, her right foot forward and pointed, her blue dress sparkling and beautiful—announcing to the whole world that she belonged with the best—she felt more like a Champion than a Novice.

As she began to move athletically, artistically, precisely across the stage, she felt the joy of it all—dancing with her best friend in her brand-new solo dress.

And her Aunt Kat was getting better!

# *Thirteen*

August.

Was it always the year's hottest month? It seemed so today, even at 7:30 in the morning. "It's not the heat, it's the humidity," her father often said, wiping the sweat from his own brow on these Wisconsin summer days. Kaylee disagreed. It was the heat *and* the humidity. And it was also the hill.

She preferred to think of it as her mountain.

She could have run toward Rosemary's downtown. That was as flat as a dance floor. But that would have been the easy way. You don't get to the top of the mountain without turning into the hill. And so she had turned away from downtown, away from the Stitchin' Kitchen when she had reached the end of Cranberry Street. She had turned left for two blocks and then another left onto Tower Court. This road twisted through a newer neighborhood built on a bluff overlooking a gravel pit. A vine-covered, rusted water tower, unused during Kaylee's lifetime, stood at the peak, the word ROSEMARY faded almost past recognition on its round side. As part of her routine, Kaylee would run to the end of the road, glance up at the tower, turn and head back toward home, a one-mile round trip.

Keep your sights on the top of the mountain, and keep climbing.

That's what Aunt Kat had said. Kaylee determined that from now on, this would be her motto.

"I'm going to qualify for Open Prizewinner in all of my dances before the end of the year!" Kaylee had announced to Caitlin one evening at dance practice as they laced on their ghillies.

Caitlin eyed her friend dubiously. "Weren't you the one quoting Clarissa Golden, telling how it would be so tough to earn firsts in all your dances in one year? Most dancers don't even get top-three finishes in all of their dances in one year!"

"So," said a familiar voice above them. Miss Helen had apparently caught their conversation. "You think you will win firsts in all your dances? What makes you better than the other girls? The ones you will be dancing against?"

Kaylee felt a bit embarrassed that Miss Helen had heard her boast, but she also felt challenged. "I want it more!"

Miss Helen nodded and almost smiled. "That is a good start. But it is not enough to simply want something. If you want to become better than the other dancers, you must be willing to do what they are not doing."

And this was what had prompted Kaylee to start running a mile every morning, to the tower and back. She added more sit-ups to her routine, too. And instead of dancing for a half-hour to an hour each day, she doubled her practice time at home.

"I wish you would have put in this much time on soccer when you were playing," her father said one night at the supper table. "You would have been a superstar."

Mrs. O'Shay frowned at her husband. "I wish she would put in this much time on homework!"

Kaylee smiled at her mother. "If homework meant medals, cool costumes and not just sitting around, maybe I would!"

Kaylee knew that her mother secretly approved whole-heartedly that she was so devoted to Irish dance. However, on the hottest day in August, Mrs. O'Shay finally kicked her daughter out the door.

"It's too hot to stay inside and dance! Why don't you and Jackie go swimming?"

Kaylee, her Trean Gaoth Academy t-shirt wet with perspiration, decided that it sounded like a pretty good idea. Donning her swimsuit, t-shirt and sandals, she hopped on her bike and met Jackie in front of the ice cream shop in the downtown. From there they pedaled to the Rosemary municipal pool overlooking the river. The large, fenced in pool had several colorful water slides at one end and a wide, concrete recreation area littered with white plastic tables and recliners. During warm weather, the place was typically packed—as it was today.

"Everybody is here!" said Jackie. "Unfortunately, there simply aren't enough boys in our school that look buff in a swimsuit."

Kaylee sighed. "They're thirteen! Almost no one looks good in a swimsuit at thirteen!"

They found an open recliner and placed their sandals and t-shirts on it. Then they splashed in the water for half an hour, finally crawling out exhausted and stretching out on towels to tan.

Kaylee had barely closed her eyes when she felt a shadow cool her. Opening them, she saw Brittany and Heather standing above. Kaylee popped into a sitting position and brought her legs underneath her in case she needed to flee. Jackie, sensing her movement, sat up, too.

"Pretty cool party, hey O'Shay?" Seeing Brittany in her cutting-edge-of-fashion yellow swimsuit, she was certain most of the boys at the pool would agree that at least one thirteen-year-old looked good in a swimsuit.

Kaylee shrugged, trying to sound as though she went to unsupervised parties that were raided by the police all the time. "It was okay."

"Everybody got away from the cops except Zack and Rachel!" continued Brittany. "Zack said he would never have gotten caught, but the cop drew his gun and threatened to shoot!"

Kaylee was tempted to tell Brittany that Zack had been so panicked that he had blundered right into the police officer. However, she bit her tongue. Brittany had not told the police or her parents that Kaylee had been at the party. Kaylee was not going to rat-out Zack for his lie. Cool people did not do that sort of thing.

"What happened to Zack and Rachel?" asked Kaylee, who was curious and who felt a bit of pity toward Rachel. "Did they get arrested?"

"Tickets for underage drinking," said Brittany. "And their parents had to come pick them up from cop land. I guess Rachel is pretty much grounded until she's twenty."

Based on how Rachel had looked at the party, Kaylee figured it was no wonder that she got caught. She probably had not even realized she had been taken to the police department until the next day.

"Was your dad mad?" Kaylee asked suddenly, remembering that Brittany had hosted the party and her punishment was likely to be worst of all.

Brittany smiled as if this were the proudest moment in any thirteen-year-old's life. "Sure. But not at me."

Kaylee felt confused. She knew how her own parents would have reacted if the cops had arrived to bust a drinking party she had hosted. "Didn't the cops give you a ticket for hosting the party?"

Brittany shook her head, and the smile became a smirk. "I carried the guitar and amp to the house and then came to the front door looking all sleepy-eyed when the cops knocked. Said I didn't know anything about a party, but that kids sometimes drank out in the woods without anyone's permission. They tried to wake my mom, but she was so far out of it that all they could get was a little mumbling and then she'd pass out again. Then my dad showed up, and he of course believed my story. So they told us to keep our eyes open and call if we noticed any more activity in the woods."

Heather laughed. "The cops in this town are so stupid!"

Only Brittany could host a party, have it busted by the police, and come away unscathed. Although Kaylee knew she could never lie to the police, she was awed by Brittany's knack for survival. And it certainly felt better being a part of Brittany's circle of comrades than being a target.

"Hey!" said Brittany suddenly. "Why don't you guys come with us? We're going to initiate the seventh graders!"

Kaylee asked what she meant.

"We're going to be the eighth graders at Kennedy Park, the leaders of the school," explained Heather.

"We've got to show the incoming seventh graders who's the boss. Put them in their place!"

Brittany pointed to the concession stand. "See that group standing in line? The first six are coming to Kennedy Park. The tall girl is Corrine Dall, who thinks she's the next big thing. Come on!"

Brittany motioned for her to follow. Kaylee looked back at Jackie, who simply rolled her eyes and shouted, "No thanks! I'm going to get something to drink."

Although torn, Kaylee swept along in Brittany's wake. It felt good not having to fight her, being on the same side. Even when they had played on the same soccer team, they had never really been on the same side.

Brittany led Heather and Kaylee to the side of the pool nearest the concessions. "Once Corrine and her friends get their food, they'll be walking right past here to get to where they're sitting on those plastic chairs." She pointed. "Their hands will be full of food. They won't see it coming at all! Sploosh!"

Kaylee stood back behind some mothers with young children, and just as Brittany had predicted, the seventh graders carrying hot dogs, pizza slices, nacho trays and soft drinks began their parade between them and the pool edge. Suddenly, Brittany shouted, "Now!" The three older girls leapt out. Heather and Brittany administered a couple of savage pushes, sending three girls—including Corrine—and two boys into the pool where they came up spluttering, wiping their faces, their food floating in the chlorinated water, their cola drinks forming clouds like octopus ink.

One girl—the one Kaylee had popped out next to—remained standing on the pool edge, her eyes wide, clutching her soft drink and nachos. She was the smallest of the six with curly hair and freckles. She reminded Kaylee of herself. In fact, the resigned and powerless expression on her face brought familiar feelings back to Kaylee. *Don't do this,* the girl's face seemed to plead.

Both Brittany and Heather shouted at the same time. "Push her!"

Kaylee did. The girl tumbled backwards, pinching her eyes shut, the nachos and soda pop flying into the chlorine soup. A part of her felt a kind of exhilaration, the sort that one must get when bungee jumping, she thought. It was if she had stepped off a cliff and enjoyed a moment of intense thrill. She heard Brittany's voice: "Yeah!" And Heather's: "All right!"

Then the moment dissolved as she saw the frustration, embarrassment and anger on the faces of the seventh graders bobbing in the water, and as she registered the stern countenances of the parents seated nearby. She had seen this look before; adults had expressions they reserved for the "good" kids, and a completely different, narrow-eyed, set-jaw, full-of-judgement-and-wrath look for the "bad" kids as judged by their ill-mannered behaviors and appearance.

This was the "bad" look.

Then a voice boomed out behind her. "All right, you three! Let's go!"

It was the adult pool supervisor, and in a moment, Heather, Brittany and Kaylee stood outside the chain link fence surrounding the municipal pool—banned for the rest of the summer.

"It was worth it," laughed Heather. "To see the look on their faces!"

"The summer's almost over anyway!" shrugged Brittany. Then she and Heather turned toward the street.

Calling over her shoulder toward Kaylee, she asked, "Are you coming?"

Kaylee shook her head, and turned back toward the pool. She immediately saw Jackie standing back near the plastic chairs, staring out at Kaylee, her face sad and troubled.

And Kaylee wondered what she was doing on the wrong side of the fence.

# Fourteen

Where did the summer go?

Dance, dance and hearts beat faster. A two-part beat, thunder and echo, like two armies, Passion and Art, marching toward each other on the battlefield, their steps increasing in speed, intensity.

Stop. Water break. Yes, it's hot for June. The air conditioning is on. But it works better when it's cooler outside. Like below 75 degrees.

But can't let the heat stop us. Back onto the dance floor. With the music now. Good. Toes pointed. Arch! Back row, stay in time!

Only two months until the big Irish festival at the lakefront. Thousands of people. Tens of thousands! A hundred thousand! More! They'll be watching you up on that stage, so you'd better know your steps! Let's go again now!

Practice at home, too! Do the stretching! Get those kicks high! Fifteen minutes a day. Twenty. An hour. Two. You'll never be a champion unless you outwork the other girls. Practice in your bedroom . . . living room . . . basement . . . Maybe dad will build you a dance floor. And there's always the driveway. Just practice.

And eat healthy.

Can't go to the beach today, guys. I've got a feis. A dance competition. ChicagoMinneapolisDallasSeattle. Maybe next weekend. Oops, sorry! Cleveland next week! Let's try July.

Dance, dance and hearts beat faster. A two-part beat, thunder and echo, like two armies, Passion and Art, marching toward each other on the battlefield, their steps increasing in speed, intensity.

Didn't place in my reel.

Hornpipe.

Treble jig.

Keep trying! Don't give up! Practice makes perfect!

Didn't place in my traditional set.

One and two and turn and step! Keep going! I know you're tired, but practice will be over in another hour. It's another hot one! Wipe the sweat out of your eyes! All right, get a drink of water and meet back here on the dance floor in five!

My brother says his football team doesn't train this hard!

Your brother's football team isn't competing against athletes from seventeen states and Canada!

One and two and leap!

Dance, dance and hearts beat faster. A two-part beat, thunder and echo, like two armies, Passion and Art, marching toward each other on the battlefield, their steps increasing in speed, intensity.

I got a fifth in my slip jig!

A fourth in my hornpipe!

Dance until your parents tell you to stop making all that noise and go to sleep. Dance until you wear holes in those ghillies.  Dance until you wear the finish off the wooden floor in your living room.

Just dance!

Only a month until the big summer show!  We want to be perfect!  Let's do it again!

Sure, I'd love to go to a movie tonight.  But I've got to get to bed early.  We're leaving for Chicago at five.  Big feis in the Windy City.

Maybe next week.  Oops!  Sorry!  Next week is Nashville!

I got a bronze!  Third place!

Sit-ups.  Tighten those abs!  Are you practicing at home?  Stretching?  Get those kicks higher!  Keep the arms straight!

And I thought June was hot!

It must be ninety in here!  Open a door!  Open a window!  Open all the windows!

But keep dancing!

Two weeks until the big summer show!  We're not nearly ready!  From now on, we'll be practicing an extra half-hour!

Where's Gabrielle?  What?  She quit?

She said dance got boring.  She had other stuff to do.  Had to get a job.

But that wasn't the real reason.

Couldn't take it.  Didn't have the stuff.

If it was easy, anyone could do it!

Only a week to go!  We've got to get it right!  Let's try it again.  Two more times!  Three times!  Six!  Ten!

Do you have to dance right here?  I'm trying to watch TV.

Practice-practice-practice.

It's showtime! I didn't think there would be so many people!

Kicks high! Toes pointed! Hold those leaps! Yes! Right on beat! Looking good!

The crowd was on its feet! You nailed it! What a performance!

Only two more shows.

Dance, dance and hearts beat faster.

Maybe time for one more feis. Miami? Portland? Pittsburgh? Little Rock?

Silver medal.

But I wanted gold!

Someday.

Keep at it. The battle is often won by those who persevere. By those who dream of

Gold.

Ring-ring! Alarm clock sounds. School bell tolls. Welcome back.

The dream goes on.

Dance, dance and hearts beat faster. A two-part beat, thunder and echo, like two armies, Passion and Art, marching toward each other on the battlefield, their steps increasing in speed, intensity.

Where did the summer go?

# Fifteen

Keep your sights on the top of the mountain, and keep climbing.

"Only a quarter mile to go, Kaylee!" called Aunt Kat breathlessly. "We can do this!"

Kaylee could see the finish line. She felt tired, but not completely wrecked. Other runners near them began to pick up the pace, making the final push to the banner. Kaylee felt herself responding competitively. "Come on, Aunt Kat! Let's see how many people we can pass before the finish!"

For a moment, Aunt Kat's face reflected doubt, but she pumped her arms faster and stuck with her niece who passed one, then another, then a group of three. Finally they cruised beneath the red and white FINISH banner and into a narrow chute lined with colorful pennants where volunteers tore off the data tags from their competitor numbers.

Once they had emerged from the finish chute, Aunt Kat gasped for breath, her hands on her knees. Kaylee found that she felt pretty good and went to a nearby table to grab a cup of water and a banana for Aunt Kat and herself. When she returned, Aunt Kat was still bent over.

Kaylee offered her the cup, which she took, and after another few moments, Aunt Kat stood and sipped.

"I've walked two miles, but it's been a long time since I've run that far," said Aunt Kat.

The farthest Kaylee had run in her previous workouts was a mile and a half. However, Aunt Kat had asked her if she wanted to run in the Paavo Community Hospital Run. "All the money raised goes to cancer research," Aunt Kat had said. That was all Kaylee had needed to hear, not simply because it was for a good cause, but mostly because it was something she could do with Aunt Kat.

"You hardly look tired!" said Aunt Kat, still breathing hard.

"I guess all the training I've been doing lately is paying off," said Kaylee, smiling.

Miss Helen had noticed it in dance practice, too. "You seem to have more energy," she said one evening at Trean Gaoth Academy. "And your jumps are higher, more athletic."

Aunt Kat's progress over the summer had been extraordinary, too. Two months earlier, she had felt weak, tired, frequently sick. She still appeared frightfully thin and a colorful bandana covered the top of her head. But in August, the doctors had said that it looked like her treatments were progressing well. Now she had just finished a two-mile run.

"If you work hard, you can overcome any obstacle," Kaylee had told April Lee in dance class one night. "That's what my aunt taught me."

Hundreds of runners stood on the grass near the Paavo Community Hospital parking lot, chatting and sipping sport drinks.    Kaylee and Aunt Kat weaved through them toward Aunt Kat's car.

"I think we should stop for ice cream on the way home," said Aunt Kat as they buckled themselves in. "Today, we earned it!"

On Tuesday, school started, and in Kaylee's opinion, the first day was a complete waste of time. Every class was exactly the same:

- Put students into an alphabetical seating chart (Kaylee always ended up somewhere in the middle of the room; just once it would have been nice to sit in the back).
- Hand out textbooks.
- Discuss the classroom rules, 98% of which were the same for every class.

"Why didn't they just send us our seating charts and a copy of the rules in the mail and let us sleep late one final time?" asked Jackie when she caught up to her friend just outside the lunch room between classes.

"This day is a total bore," admitted Kaylee. "But you've got to agree, this year is going to be cool. We own this school! We're the eighth graders!"

"This year is going to be awful," moped Jackie. "You and I have different lunch periods! And Angelo Zizzo may need to have surgery!"

As Kaylee brainstormed ways that she might take her friend's mind off the Angelo Zizzo Crisis, Brittany and Heather passed on the other side of the hallway.

"Hey, O'Shay!" called Brittany, carrying a single spiral notebook in contrast to Kaylee's armful of textbooks. "Sweet time at the pool!"

Kaylee smiled weakly.

Brittany leaned closer. "There's a big party tonight. Sort of an end-of-summer thing. My place again."

Kaylee had no desire to attend another of Brittany's parties. She felt guilty for having misled her parents about the last one. They would have been horrified to know that there were cigarettes, alcohol and no adult supervision. In addition, Kaylee had felt bad about they way they had all treated Rachel—although in her opinion, Rachel had not shown a superfluity of brain cells, either. Perhaps it would not always be this way, Kaylee thought, but right now, her idea of a good party was her best friends and sleeping bags packed together on someone's bedroom floor, telling jokes, sharing their dreams and talking about the cute boys at Kennedy Park Middle School.

Or even talking about Angelo Zizzo.

Kaylee was about to say no to the offer, but instead she heard herself ask a question: "Can Jackie come, too!"

She cast a sideways glance and saw her friend's eyebrows arch in alarm.

Brittany seemed at a loss for words, although she quickly recovered and looked as if she might give grudging approval. However, Heather spoke before she had a chance.

"She wouldn't fit in."

Kaylee glared into Heather's face. "Why not?"

Heather's mouth twisted into a cruel smile. "Our parties aren't for losers."

As always, Jackie was quick with a reply. "Then why does Brittany invite you?"

Heather's expression grew dangerous. "You'd better watch your back on the soccer field this fall, Fortune Cookie!"

Jackie took a step forward. "Is that a threat?"

Kaylee followed.  "You can't talk to my friend like that!"

Brittany looked them over for a moment and then shook her head. "Come on, Heather.  O'Shrimp would obviously rather play with dolls and have pillow fights than go to a real party."

*As a matter of fact*, Kaylee thought to herself as Heather took a step backward, *that does sound like a lot of fun.*

As Brittany and Heather drifted through the cafeteria doors, Kaylee nudged her friend. "You okay?"

Jackie opened her mouth to answer when a voice boomed out: "Hey losers!"

On reflex, Kaylee and Jackie turned toward the sound and immediately were hit with a shower of catsup flipped in their direction from about ten feet away by Brittany and Heather, using plastic spoons.

"Told you they'd look!" laughed Heather, and half of the students in the crowded hallway joined in.  Brittany laughed, too, and then the duo turned and half-jogged back toward the tables.

Jackie rushed inside, grabbed several napkins and began dabbing at the red sauce on her face and arms.  "I don't know about you, but right now, I don't really feel like I *own* this school."

Kaylee dabbed her face with her own napkin, but noticed that the catsup had splattered her t-shirt as well. *Oh no! Catsup stains!*

Her *Isle of Green Fire* t-shirt.  The special one that Caitlin had gotten her for her birthday.

And now catsup covered Elena McGinty's autograph.

# Sixteen

Mrs. Hubbard inched the van along the metal ramp at about half a mile per hour.

"You can go faster, Mom!" said Caitlin impatiently. "Hundreds of cars go across this thing every day!"

Her mother's eyes darted back and forth from the ramp to the swirling water visible through the metal grate. Then, after very nearly forever, the car was in the hold of the ferry and Mrs. Hubbard had been directed to a parking spot by one of the attendants.

Mrs. Hubbard, Mrs. O'Shay, Grandma Birdsall and Aunt Kat exited the van and then waited for the two jabbering thirteen-year-olds. Leaving most of their luggage locked in the vehicle, they made their way up steps to the upper level of the boat, moving slowly to accommodate Grandma Birdsall's irregular gait and frequent stops to catch her breath.

"This will be fun!" said Mrs. Hubbard as they finally emerged on the passenger deck and found seats in an enclosed area that looked to Kaylee like a cross between a fast food restaurant and the passenger cabin of an airplane. Blue, cushioned seats three deep lined the windows on each side of the wide room, and an even wider row of seats positioned around tables occupied the center. "We can sit back, relax, and enjoy the trip!"

They found seats together, chatted excitedly for a minute and then heard the deep blatting tone of the ship's horn.

"I don't know why we're sitting here," said Aunt Kat, rising. "We might as well be sitting at home! I'm going up top!"

Kaylee and Caitlin followed as Kat exited at the rear of the room. They found themselves on a wide platform overlooking the stern of the vessel. Below, they could see several cars protruding from the hold. White water churned by the ship's engines roiled behind the boat. Turning from this scene, they climbed stairs leading to the viewing deck atop the room they had just left.

A gray, flat expanse greeted them, surrounded on all sides by a white metal railing. Dozens of others had come up to this deck to enjoy the start of the journey. On Kaylee's right, the Milwaukee skyline rose in the distance, falling behind them gradually as the ferry droned to the east. Kaylee whirled and noticed that they had almost reached the narrow gap in the breakwater with the rolling blue waters of Lake Michigan beyond. A few sailboats skimmed the waves, and here and there, a motorized boat as well. As they left the breakwater behind, the ferry suddenly gained speed, and the wind hit them as though they were standing on the roof of a car racing down the freeway.

"Isn't this great?" shouted Caitlin.

Kaylee nodded energetically and Aunt Kat added, "Sure beats driving through Chicago traffic!"

Driving through Chicago traffic had been the original plan. South through Chicago, then north to

Holland, Michigan on the east side of the lake for the Holland Feis.

"Why don't you take the ferry to Muskegon with us?" Mrs. Hubbard had suggested. "It's just a short drive from Muskegon to Holland, and from what I've heard, it's a beautiful trip!"

Of course Mrs. O'Shay had initially refused on the grounds that it would be far too expensive to go by ferry. Then Aunt Kat had stepped in.

Aunt Kat seemed to be stepping in a lot lately.

She had helped pay for Kaylee's solo dress, too. And, of course, the trip to Ireland.

"They talk about how artists are always starving," Kaylee had confided to Caitlin once. "But my aunt is rolling in it! Her paintings and stuff must be worth a fortune!"

The two mothers had now appeared behind the girls.

"Looks like the lake is pretty calm," said Mrs. Hubbard.

Kaylee's mother nodded. "Even if it was hailing cantaloupes and the waves were ten feet high, it sure beats driving through Chicago!"

Kaylee leaned close to Caitlin. "You can sure tell they're sisters."

"Hey," said Caitlin suddenly, "let's dance!"

The two young girls moved into the center of the deck and began their reel. Several other girls who were apparently crossing on the ferry to dance at the Holland Feis joined in.

Aunt Kat laughed. "With those two, everything's a dance stage!"

"Sometimes it seems like the judges must just draw names out of a hat!"

Kaylee's mother often said things like this following a trip to the results posters at a feis. As Kaylee's dances were underway, Mrs. O'Shay would watch her daughter, but she would also try to determine which of the other dancers looked good. Occasionally, she would jot down their competitor numbers to see whether the judges saw it the same way. Sometimes they did. Other times, Mrs. O'Shay found herself way off the mark.

And there were times when she felt certain that Kaylee had nailed a dance, only to find that the judge had issued her daughter a fourth- or fifth-place—or no place at all.

It was easy for her mother—and, occasionally, for Kaylee—to become frustrated with the judging. Once they had seen an elderly judge doze off during a dance. Eight dancers passed in front of him before he woke up to the final pair, smiled at the group as if nothing had happened, and jotted down his "scores".

And there were judges who seemed to have their minds made up before a person even danced, keeping his eyes on only one dancer in a pair, as if the other did not exist.

Of course, Kaylee knew that the vast majority of judges were good, competent individuals who did their best to render fair and appropriate decisions. However, the rare instance of apparent partiality or laziness seemed to make judges convenient scapegoats when a dancer had a bad day at a feis.

Then there were days when nothing seemed to matter.

Days when a dancer felt so right that her feet seemed not to merely follow the music, but to derive their power from it. Days when there was no need to think or hope, only to dance.

Days when a dancer was so on, that no one could sleep through or ignore her performance.

That was how Kaylee felt at the Holland Feis in Michigan.

"Mom, I know I nailed that slip jig!" she said after finishing her last dance.

"You looked good," agreed Mrs. O'Shay. "But remember, it's difficult to predict how the judges will score you."

"I felt really good today, too!" said Caitlin. "Maybe by the end of the day, I'll be qualified for Open in as many dances as Kaylee!"

As the two returned to their camping area to change out of their dresses and into their jam pants and t-shirts, Kaylee noticed Aunt Kat napping in one of the folding chairs, her omnipresent sketch book face down across her like a tiny blanket. I'm the one who should feel tired, thought Kaylee. She felt tempted to take a peek at what her aunt had been sketching but resisted, fearing that she might wake Aunt Kat.

They knew the last of their results would not yet be posted, and so they wandered, eventually finding themselves in front of the PC stage. Riley waved from the check-in area, and so the girls stayed to watch him dance.

"He's amazing!" said Caitlin.

"Yeah," said Kaylee wistfully, and Caitlin punched her playfully in the shoulder.

"I've just got my hard shoe dance to finish," explained Riley afterwards. "When you're in PC and you only have two dances and recalls, your day goes quickly."

"We didn't know you were going to be here," said Kaylee.

"My mom and I came over yesterday on the ferry," Riley explained.

Kaylee's eyes widened a bit. "We didn't see you!"

The reason, they discovered, was that Riley had come over on an earlier boat. "But it looks like we'll be heading back to Milwaukee together!" he said after Kaylee revealed when they would be leaving.

Better than two hours on a boat with a boy who understood Irish dance and was very nearly as cute as Michael Black. That, thought Kaylee, was the sweetest end to a feis she would ever experience.

And then, when she and Caitlin arrived at the results, it got a bit sweeter still.

First place in the slip jig was listed as number 477. That was Kaylee's number.

"I'm in Open Prizewinner in everything!" squealed Kaylee.

Caitlin offered a wide smile. "Great."

As it turned out, Caitlin had earned a second and two thirds—a pretty good feis. However, Kaylee understood her lack of enthusiasm instantly. Caitlin was still qualified for Open Prizewinner in only one dance.

"It'll all come in time," said Kaylee kindly. "Just keep working hard. That's what Aunt Kat says. With hard work and a positive attitude, you can do anything!"

"Yeah." The wide smile again.

On the late afternoon ferry, Aunt Kat bought chicken wraps and chocolate chip cookies from the grill.

Then Caitlin leaned onto her mother's shoulder and fell asleep.

"She's been quiet all afternoon," whispered Mrs. Hubbard. "I hope she's not coming down with anything."

Kaylee excused herself and went to the top deck again. It did not take her long to find what she was looking for.

Or rather, whom.

"I heard you had quite a day!" said Riley, leaning against the rail next to her. Kaylee felt an exhilaration that might have had something to do with the spray of the lake that played across her freckled cheeks—or which, perhaps, might have been caused by something altogether different.

"I did okay."

Riley coughed. "Okay? You're Open in all of your dances! Four more first place finishes and you're in PC, just like me!"

Kaylee tried, without much success, to stifle her smile. "Getting first places in Open Prizewinner is going to be a lot more difficult than in Novice."

"First place finishes are tough at every level," said Riley, and for awhile, they simply leaned upon the railing, watching the enormous starboard pontoon slice through the water.

"So," said Kaylee after a long pause, "how do you spend your time when you're not at feiseanna?"

Riley chuckled. "Practicing for feiseanna! But I also play baseball in the summer leagues. And I read. Science fiction, mostly."

Kaylee wrinkled her nose at this.

"I'm thinking of going out for football next year in high school," he continued. "And I'm addicted to

Asunder." When he saw her confused look, he explained. "It's a video game. My mom thinks it's rotting my brain."

Kaylee nodded. "Don't tell my brother about it. He's constantly saving the universe. Or destroying it. Whatever you do with those games. On the other hand, his brain is pretty rotten already."

"Maybe I can meet him sometime," said Riley. "Sounds like we have a lot in common."

Kaylee shuddered at the thought. "What about you? Any brothers or sisters?"

Riley shook his head. "It's just me and my mom. My dad died when I was six."

"I'm sorry," said Kaylee quietly.

"I remember him playing with me. We had little metal cars and blocks and we'd build cities. I really miss him sometimes. Especially at feiseanna. It would have been nice if he could have seen me dance."

As the sun began to dip toward the horizon, they went back to watching the water churn away from the hull. And it seemed to Kaylee as if Riley had moved a little bit closer to her.

"Oh!" said Kaylee suddenly. "I forgot to ask how you finished!"

Riley held up two fingers. "Second. It's not bad, but I usually beat the guy who finished ahead of me." After a pause, he asked, "And what about your friend?"

"Caitlin? A second and two thirds. A really good day. But she didn't seem too excited."

Riley asked how many dances before Caitlin would be in Open in everything. When Kaylee told him three, he nodded as if this seemed to make sense.

"She's probably having a tough time with it, seeing you moving up a little faster."

"But she's so close!  She places high in almost every dance!"

"Sure," agreed Riley.  "But it's still gotta be tough. Think of how you would feel if you were in Open in one dance, but Caitlin had qualified in all four."

Kaylee suddenly felt uncomfortable.  "Are you saying that you think it's okay for Caitlin to be all moody and crabby about it?"

"I'm just saying it's not so hard to imagine what she's going through," said Riley amiably.

"Well," said Kaylee, feeling irritated now, "I can't imagine it.  I know she wants to make Open, but that doesn't give her the right to be mad at me."

Riley nodded, and the worried look in his eyes suggested that he was now scrambling to find a way out of this conversation.  "You're right.  She shouldn't be mad at anyone.  But you told me all she's really done so far is ignore you all afternoon.  Maybe the whole thing will blow over if you don't make a big deal about it."

Kaylee's eyes widened and her jaw tightened. "You think I'm making a big deal about it?"  Why was Riley taking Caitlin's side?  It made her angrier and angrier.  "You think this is happening because I'm being too sensitive?  Caitlin's the one acting immature, not me!"

Riley held up his hands.  "I'm not trying to start a fight.  I just thought maybe you should give Caitlin a break.  I'm sure you both could have handled things differently."

"All I did was dance my best and qualify for Open!" said Kaylee, her eyes narrowing murderously. "What should I have done differently?  Danced barefoot so I'd get a lower score?  Wear my wig sideways?"

Riley did not say anything. Instead, he leaned over the railing once more and stared out at the water.

Kaylee knew that she had allowed herself to become too upset, but she could not help it. It hurt so badly to think that one of her best friends, Caitlin, could turn away from her. Somehow this made Riley's attitude seem all the more treasonous. She wanted to find words that would restore them to the place they had been only a few minutes ago, but now she could not trust herself to say anything on the chance that she might make the situation a hundred times worse. Before she had a chance, her mother appeared on the deck.

"Just came up to check on you, sweetheart."

Riley turned from the rail, struggled to put on a more pleasant face. Kaylee awkwardly mumbled an introduction.

"I think I've seen you at the feises before," said Mrs. O'Shay. Aunt Kat, who had come up behind her mother gave Kaylee a big wink and a You Go Girl smile. Thankfully, Riley chose the moment to excuse himself to check on the whereabouts of his own mother.

Mrs. O'Shay turned into the wind and drank in the fresh air. "When you stand right in the wind, it's pretty cold. Do you want your jacket?"

Kaylee, who had not noticed the coolness of the air until that moment, shook her head.

They stood together for a few minutes before Mrs. O'Shay surrendered, stating that she was heading back inside where it was warmer.

"Is Caitlin still sleeping?" asked Kaylee.

"No," said Mrs. O'Shay. "She's reading a book."

Kaylee thought about what Riley had said but offered no comment to her mother.

As Mrs. O'Shay retreated, Aunt Kat, wrapped in a heavy winter jacket, sidled close.

"Sorry about our poor timing."

Kaylee felt her cheeks warm. "He's just a friend."

Aunt Kat feigned surprise. "An incredibly hot friend! I guess this Irish dance stuff has its perks."

Now Kaylee smiled despite herself. Her mother would have never used the word "hot" in reference to a boy that her little girl might be interested in. That was why she liked Aunt Kat—she was like her mother, but then again, she wasn't.

A mile of waves passed beneath them.

"I was wondering," said Aunt Kat suddenly, "if you would mind if we made a little change in our Ireland plans."

Kaylee's head snapped around. "Oh no! We're not canceling the trip, are we?"

"Of course not," said her aunt.

"Or putting it off even farther in the future?"

"No," said Aunt Kat. "I just happened to get a pretty good deal on some tickets around Christmas vacation time. You and Will have about two weeks off, so you wouldn't miss any school."

Christmas break? That was only three months off rather than the seven months that needed to be slogged through until spring break.

"Oh, Aunt Kat, that would be great!"

Aunt Kat smiled, and in the direct light of the setting sun, Kaylee realized for the first time how much she looked like her own mother, Grandma Birdsall.

"I figured you might say that," said Kat, and then she pulled her niece to her in an enormous hug that surprised Kaylee with its ferocity. After that, she clutched her jacket tighter and exited in the same direction that Kaylee's mother had gone.

Kaylee wanted to stay on the top deck until the sun had set, to let the greatness of this place and the events of the day swirl around her. She had qualified for Open in every dance. Riley had stood close to her on the top deck. The trip to Ireland with her aunt had been moved closer by four months. It was the kind of day where a person should celebrate. A day for joyful yells and hugs. A day to be proud. A day to feel loved, to feel content, to feel like a champion.

Somehow these feelings eluded Kaylee. It was as if they were mere shadows about to be lost in the total darkness of a setting sun.

And all she felt was the growing coldness as night descended over Lake Michigan.

# *Seventeen*

The excitement of the new school year lasted approximately two weeks. Then the student body at Kennedy Park Middle School settled into its role of rebellious complacency. People talked about how unfair or impossible Mr. or Mrs. So-and-so's tests were, gossiped about the relationship barometers of the Powerful and Popular, and enthused about the athletic performances of teen deities like Michael Black, who quarterbacked the eighth-grade tackle football team, or Brittany Hall, who was mentioned whenever soccer, volleyball or anything else involving athleticism became fodder for conversation.

The Holland Feis had coincided with this ebb in spirit, and now the middle schoolers had to look forward to specific calendar events to break up the routine drudgery of their young lives.

"If I can just make it to the last week in October," said Jackie as they paused in the hallway, "I think I'll be okay. That's when we get a four-day weekend for teachers to have their big convention in Milwaukee. Then it's just a short jump to Thanksgiving, and another short jump to Christmas vacation! After that, the year's half over!"

Kaylee was more excited about Christmas vacation than she had ever been.

Ireland!

Would it be snowing there? Would they celebrate Christmas the same way that her family did in the States? She had so many questions and had not yet gotten a chance to ask her Aunt Kat or to conduct research in books or online.

Of course, before Ireland, two feiseanna remained, one in October and another in November.

"That rug in your room definitely has to go!" said Mrs. O'Shay one day, watching Kaylee practicing—and almost tripping over one of the growing number of worn spots. "With all the dancing you do on it, it's hardly more than a thin blanket! But I just don't have the energy to do anything about it right now."

"What's under my rug?" Kaylee asked one night at supper.

Her father shrugged. "Probably just wood."

Kaylee's eyes widened. "What are you going to do with my carpet after it's out of my room?"

Her father had looked at Kaylee as if she were insane. "Do with it? Stuff the pieces of that rag in our trash can!"

The next night—which Kaylee probably should have been devoting to a more polished final draft of a paper for Mrs. Morrissey's English class—she tore out the carpet herself and found a worn but solid plank floor.

"I wish I'd done this years ago!" she said to her father. "It's perfect for dancing! Except for being small, that is."

When her mother arrived home later, she looked tired but impressed with her daughter's handiwork. "I'm sorry I couldn't help you, honey. I've just been so busy with the Stitchin' Kitchen, helping your Aunt Kat and driving your grandmother around."

"Where's Grandma been going?" asked Kaylee.

"She's been spending the days over at Aunt Kat's," said Mrs. O'Shay.

Since Kaylee had been in school during the day, she really had not noticed her grandmother's absence. And she had seen less of Aunt Kat, too. But it certainly made sense for Aunt Kat to look after her grandmother during the day, considering Grandma Birdsall's heart problems and the fact that both of them would have just been sitting alone in separate houses.

"Since your grandmother needs a good night's sleep," said Mrs. O'Shay, "no hard shoes after nine!"

Still, her mother consented to a Saturday sleepover with Caitlin. "Grandma Birdsall can stay at Aunt Kat's. But that doesn't mean you can stay up all night!"

Caitlin had seemed somewhat aloof in recent weeks. Kaylee accepted Riley's explanation for this, but she knew that sooner or later, her friend would bounce back. After all, one of them was bound to progress a little faster than the other. It might, as Riley had said, have been Caitlin. Eventually, Caitlin would be at the Open Prizewinner level in all of her dances, too. Surely her friend understood this.

At dance class on Thursday, Kaylee suggested the sleepover. "You should see my floor! It sounds like you're at a feis when you dance hard shoes on it now!"

"I'm busy this weekend," Caitlin said curtly, and then Kaylee endured one of her most awkward practices at Trean Gaoth Academy, feeling as though she were simultaneously ten feet and ten thousand miles from her friend.

It did not help when Miss Helen stopped by after practice when Kaylee was pulling on her street shoes.

"So now you are Open Prizewinner in everything!"

Kaylee wished Miss Helen would speak less loudly. She could imagine Caitlin rolling her eyes as she changed shoes behind her.

"I think maybe it's time you had some extra lessons each week," continued her teacher. "This will get you prepared to move into PC."

Just hearing somebody who understood dance mention Preliminary Championship when talking to her sent a thrill up Kaylee's spine. She immediately felt guilty, knowing how overhearing this conversation must make Caitlin feel.

Miss Helen took out a card and wrote down a couple of times slots, handing it to Kaylee. "Let me know next week if either of these will work. You are starting to show me something, Miss Kaylee. Perhaps you will someday show us all!"

Even after Miss Helen moved off to talk with other dancers, Kaylee could not bring herself to turn around for a long time, fearing that Caitlin's eyes would be searing holes through her. When she finally did, Caitlin was gone.

Kaylee wished that she could make her friend feel better. However, she felt somewhat angry, too. Sure, Caitlin wanted to be in Open in all of her dances. Both of them had wanted this. But if Caitlin had reached the goal first, Kaylee felt certain she would have congratulated her friend and felt nothing but happiness for her.

She imagined Caitlin jumping joyfully next to the results wall at the Holland Feis, celebrating because she had earned the gold medals she needed to move into Open in all of her dances. Kaylee imagined herself with only a first place in one dance, knowing that in the next feis she would be dancing three Novice steps while her best friend moved on to Open in everything. She saw herself smiling, giving Caitlin a hug. Even though she was only imagining this scene, it was difficult for Kaylee to deal with the thought that she might be left behind. Suddenly she understood more completely how Caitlin felt.

*But I still wouldn't act as mean as Caitlin's acting,* Kaylee told herself, wondering at the same time whether this was really true.

Kaylee's father drove her home from practice. She tried to forget about Caitlin for awhile, telling herself that it would all sort itself out. She even talked about soccer with her father to try and distract herself. He was coaching the Bullets—Will's team—again this year, and they had won all four of their league games and finished second in a tournament in Milwaukee. As she listened to her father rave about Will's improvement, about his goal in the last game, about the team's chances of winning the league title, she felt a twinge of remorse inflicted by the memories of when her father had been her coach.

She had been improving as a player. Her team, the Green Storm, had won the league title. She had enjoyed spending time with her dad. And then she had danced away from him.

"Why do things have to change?" she asked her father suddenly.

Tom O'Shay glanced at his passenger but quickly returned his gaze to the road. "What do you mean?"

What she really meant was difficult to put into words. Why couldn't she just wrap her arms around Caitlin and her father and Jackie and Aunt Kat and everyone who she loved and simply hold onto them so that they would never drift off, never leave this place and this moment?  Ten years from now—twenty, even—why couldn't there still be sleepovers and feises and Saturday morning soccer games and her little room with the perfect dance floor and everybody smiling as she blew out the candles on her birthday cake?

She settled for, "My life was so much simpler when I was twelve!  Why can't it be like that now?"

Her father started to laugh, and this only upset Kaylee more.  When he saw the look on her face, he collected himself.

"Life's not a photograph.  It moves and changes.  Our world would be pretty dull if it was the same thing day after day."

This was the sort of thing she had expected her father to say.  It was the sort of thing grownups were always saying, and it did nothing to satisfy her.  "Don't you ever miss the way it was when you were twelve?"

Tom O'Shay thought about this for a moment.  "I miss Saturday morning cartoons."

Kaylee's mouth fell open slightly as she turned toward him.  "You used to watch cartoons?"

"Not the same ones they have on TV today.  They were better when I was a kid.  And I miss my mother making me waffles.  And my tree house."

Kaylee settled back into her seat.  "It's junk that it can't stay that way."

Her father smiled gently.  "I don't think I'd want it to be like that forever."

"But doesn't life get more crazy and difficult as you get older?"

"Sure," agreed her father.  "But along with all that craziness come some things that really make it worth the trouble, things that are a thousand times better than waffles and tree houses."

"Like what?" asked Kaylee.

Her father took one hand off the steering wheel and placed it gently on top of one of her own. And for the first time in a long time, she felt better—a thousand times better—than waffles and treehouses and even cartoons. And she wondered if, at some point in the future, life would offer her something even more wonderful and incredible than Irish dance.

When they bustled into the kitchen of their house on Cranberry Street, her father moved to the refrigerator to begin the process of preparing dinner. Kaylee, however, immediately spotted the note on the kitchen counter.

*We're at the hospital in Paavo. Will is with us.*

Her father sighed, and Kaylee knew it was because they had just driven from Paavo. "It would really be great to have cell phones!"

They had made this trip before. Three years ago, her grandmother had passed out and ended up in Paavo Community Hospital. They had diagnosed her heart condition and had started her on medication. However, there had been a couple of episodes since then.

Her mother's note had offered no specifics, but if her grandmother had been in danger of dying, Kaylee was certain it would have been worded much differently. *Grandma suffered a major heart attack* or *Please hurry.* She expected to walk into the hospital room and see her grandmother sitting up in bed, smiling as usual, laughing at all the fuss being made over nothing at all.

On the other hand, what if the suddenness of her grandmother's attack had not permitted her mother to write more?  What if the situation were far more serious this time?

Kaylee folded her hands across the seat belt and offered a silent prayer.  *Please don't let my grandmother die.* She thought of the solo dress that would remain unfinished if her grandmother were dead and quickly pushed this selfish notion from her mind.  *Please let her be okay.*

Kaylee's father stepped to the information desk in the hospital lobby.  Kaylee drifted off to one side near the elevator hallway.  It seemed to take her father an unusually long time at the desk, and when he turned back toward Kaylee, he wore an expression of grave concern.

*Oh no,* thought Kaylee.  *It's worse than I thought!* She began another silent prayer as they rode the elevator. *Please let Grandma get better!  Please let Grandma get better!*

They stepped off the elevator into a section of the hospital Kaylee had never visited before, which she interpreted as another bad sign.  Tom O'Shay squinted at plastic signs near the ceiling that indicated which room numbers were down which hallways, and after a short walk, they found themselves at room 3009.  Kaylee's father reached and gave his daughter's hand a squeeze—another bad sign.  She held her breath as they rounded the door, and there sat her grandmother, a gentle smile on her face. "Hello sweetheart," said Grandma Birdsall softly, but something was wrong with this picture.  Her grandmother sat in a chair holding the hand of the person in the bed.

And that person was Aunt Kat.

# Eighteen

Normally, Kaylee took her bike when she traveled past Rosemary's downtown. Going to Jackie's or Aunt Kat's or the beach, those were long distances, too long to travel comfortably by foot. But nothing was normal anymore. Normal had made its exit that night in the hospital.

She ran. Faster than her usual training pace. She cruised along, her arms pumping, hardly aware of the exertion.

Two weeks earlier, she had been shocked to find her aunt in a hospital bed. Aunt Kat had given an embarrassed wave as Kaylee had entered the room with her father. "Hi, Munchkin. Pretty crummy way to spend a Thursday night, hey?"

Propped into a sitting position by pillows and the bed tilt, her aunt had worn the typical hospital gown and plastic wrist bracelet. More worrisome, however, were the tubes connected to her. One seemed to carry clear fluid from an overhead bag into her arm. Another descended from her nostrils to a bedside apparatus that was beyond Kaylee's understanding. Will had sat in a chair near Grandma Birdsall while Kaylee's mother had stood on the opposite side of the bed.

And then the talking and hugging and crying had begun.

Aunt Kat's cancer had spread.

There had been some bleeding. She had taken a fall.

Now there would be more tests and more treatments, maybe even an experimental drug.

"It's bad, isn't it?" Kaylee had asked. No one had responded, but no response had been necessary. Kaylee knew that no one mentioned experimental drugs unless things were unthinkably bad.

She ran on, leaving Rosemary's downtown in her dust. The cool early October air felt good against her face and in her lungs.

Her lungs. That was one of the places where Aunt Kat's cancer had spread.

She ran harder. Shorts, running shoes, her navy blue Trean Gaoth sweatshirt, a pink stocking cap and white cotton gloves. Kaylee looked like any other jogger one might encounter on a Rosemary backstreet. But she had never run this far before, taking a maze of detours through neighborhoods that were completely unfamiliar. Even so, she did not wonder whether she would be able to make it all the way back home.

*I can do anything! Just keep my eyes on the mountaintop!*

Aunt Kat's building came into view and a minute later Kaylee stood with her hands at her sides, breathing deeply near the bush where she had often abandoned her bicycle. There was no bike for anyone to steal today. Kaylee looked absently across the street toward Aunt Victoria's, but no light or movement indicated a human presence. Reluctant to leave the crisp, invigorating air, Kaylee nonetheless climbed the steps and ducked inside.

"You ran all that way!" said Grandma Birdsall, smiling brightly, yet clucking her tongue as she ushered Kaylee through the door. "You must be exhausted!"

Kaylee shook her head. "I'm fine."

Grandma Birdsall had been living at Aunt Kat's for well over a month. Kaylee had assumed Aunt Kat had been providing care for her elderly mother, never imagining that the opposite was true.

"Can I get you an iced tea?"

"Water is good," said Kaylee.

As Grandma Birdsall shuffled off toward the kitchen, Aunt Kat's voice called out.

"What's this? Are you training for a marathon without me?"

Her aunt sat in a twin bed in the middle of the living room, propped up by pillows. "For right now, it's the best place for me," she had told Kaylee on a previous visit. "Mom can use the bedroom, I'm closer to the bathroom, and I'm right out here where there's plenty of natural light for my art."

Grandma Birdsall had told Kaylee and her mother that Aunt Kat slept a lot. "Those new treatments really wear her down," her grandmother had revealed.

Kaylee pulled a chair next to Aunt Kat's bed. "I just felt like running."

It seemed to Kaylee that Aunt Kat looked thinner, paler even than she had a week ago. Then again, perhaps she was imagining this. Her mother had said that the doctors were optimistic about the latest treatments.

But that's what they had said in August, too.

"So," said Aunt Kat after a pause, "how's my favorite munchkin's world?"

Kaylee attempted a weak smile. "It pretty much stinks. School is boring. There's too much homework. And I have no friends."

Aunt Kat frowned. "No friends? How can that be?"

"Well," she sighed, "Caitlin is still mad because I'm in Open in all my dances and she's not. Ever since school and the fall soccer season started, I hardly ever see Jackie. And I won't see Jordi or Hannah until the next feis which is in November." *And I won't see Riley until then, either,* she thought. *And he's probably mad at me, too, after how I treated him on the ferry.*

"The Caitlin thing will work itself out," said Aunt Kat sagely. "And as for the rest, girl, haven't you ever heard of the telephone? When I was your age, mom used to have to hide the phone to keep me off of it!"

"It's true," said Grandma Birdsall, returning with the water, which Kaylee gratefully took. "I'd unplug it from the wall and hide it behind the dining room curtains. Kat never had a clue!"

Kat offered her mother a sardonic grin. "I've got news for you, Mom. We discovered the phone about a week after you started hiding it there. We'd sneak it out and plug it back in when you weren't around, then put it back behind the curtain. If you wanted us not to find it, you should have hidden it behind the canned lima beans in the pantry!"

Aunt Kat and Grandma Birdsall both laughed as though this were the greatest joke either had ever heard. Kaylee smiled and then offered a tired shrug. "Everybody chats on the computer nowadays. Except me. I must be the only kid who lives in the stone age."

Grandma Birdsall half turned toward the kitchen. "I'm going to finish making supper if you two don't mind."

After she had gone, Kaylee asked Aunt Kat how she was feeling.

"Tired, mostly," she replied wearily, but with a smile. "Sometimes I get up and paint or walk a bit or do housework. It's hard, though. My brain says, 'Get up and do something,' but my body says, 'Just lay there'."

"But," said Kaylee eagerly, "you're going to beat this. You're going to win, right?"

Aunt Kat's eyes sparkled and she seemed to break free of her illness for a moment, like a swimmer breaking the surface of a dark pond. "That's the plan, Munchkin. I'm doing my best."

Kaylee gave her aunt a hug. "How long will it take? For you to get better?"

Aunt Kat waved a hand vaguely. "Difficult to say. The treatments they have me on now last a couple more weeks. Then there will be more tests and the doctors will decide where to go from there. And the new medicine . . . that could be a long time. There could also be surgery."

"Is that why you rescheduled the trip to Ireland?" asked Kaylee. "Because you might be having surgery in the spring?"

Aunt Kat looked at her niece, her face suddenly flooded with sympathy. She took Kaylee's hand. "I've always wanted to take this trip. I especially want to take it with you. When the cancer got worse, I wanted to make sure we could go, just in case."

"In case you got too sick to travel?" Kaylee asked.

Aunt Kat touched her niece's cheek. "In case I got too sick to travel," she said slowly. "And . . . just in case."

Suddenly the meaning in Aunt Kat's words hit Kaylee, and although she said nothing, she was certain her aunt noticed her eyes suddenly going wide. Kaylee could not begin to imagine the world without her Aunt Kat in it. What a colorless, joyless place it would be. The very idea frightened her, made her almost physically sick and her eyes raced around the room, looking for something that might allow her to change the subject. They fell upon a low table covered with books and art paper, upon which rested the sketchbook that Aunt Kat had been bringing to feiseanna.

Kaylee pointed to the sketchbook, searching for an antidote to the bleak images poisoning her mind. "What are you going to do with all those pictures of dancers you've been making?"

Kat reached and picked the sketchbook off the pile. "I'll probably keep filling it with sketches. Someday I'd like to do a nice painting of an Irish dancer in costume, maybe doing a leap over. And when I'm finished with the sketchbook, I'd like you to have it."

Her aunt passed the book to Kaylee, who opened it to a point in the middle at random. The drawings, some in charcoal, some in color, beautifully captured the grace and athleticism of Irish dance. As she flipped toward the back, she noticed that almost half the pages remained blank.

"You have lots of pages left before you're finished," said Kaylee, handing the book back to her aunt. "It looks like you'll be drawing for a long, long time."

Aunt Kat looked at her niece gratefully and pulled her into a hug. "That's right, Munchkin."

# Nineteen

The end of October brought a much needed break for Kaylee—a four-day school holiday to allow her teachers to attend the state education convention. What she looked forward to most was a sleepover at Jackie's house. Since the two of them had different lunch periods this year, they sometimes hardly spoke for days at a time.

"My mom says we can order pizza," said Jackie as Kaylee threw her sleeping bag onto Jackie's bedroom floor. "And we can stay up as late as we want."

"This is going to be so great," said Kaylee, giving her friend a hug. "This has been such a crummy fall. I need some good old crazy time!"

"Yeah," agreed Jackie. "School has been even more tedious and oppressive than usual."

Kaylee nodded, but she was also thinking of Caitlin and her Aunt Kat.

"What movies are we going to watch?" asked Kaylee, digging into her duffel bag and pulling out some DVDs. "I hope you have some good ones, because I'm not so sure about these. My mom checked them out from the library. I think they were popular when she was my age."

"Maybe we can do a movie later," said Jackie. "At eight o'clock, the Italians are playing Germany!"

"I was sort of hoping for something funny, like that movie we saw in Paavo over the summer. Didn't that guy star in four or five other really wild comedies?"

"But," said Jackie excitedly, "it's Angelo Zizzo's comeback game!"

Kaylee stared blankly at her friend. "I thought you said he was hurt."

Now Jackie beamed as if a member of her family had been awarded the Medal of Honor. "He just got approval from the team doctor to play two days ago!"

Kaylee did her best to smile. "Wow. That is exciting." She took a more careful look around Jackie's room and noticed that another half of a wall had been consumed by Angelo Zizzo posters. "Where do you find all the pictures?"

Jackie twisted her head to take in the growing panorama and her smile grew wider. "I found this great on-line poster site. Posterbeast! And it's not just soccer. They've got everything!"

Jackie switched on the TV in her room, which was already tuned to the proper sports channel. "Welcome, soccer fans, to a profoundly important game between Germany and Italy, important not simply because these are two of the top teams in the world right now, but because it will mark the return of soccer icon Angelo Zizzo after a lengthy absence due to injury."

"Yes!" cried Jackie as if she were actually in the cheering crowd at the stadium. "Zizzo is the king!"

A second announcer with a slightly deeper voice chimed in. "It's important for the Italians to get this win tonight, because it doesn't get any easier for them. After this, it's on to Ireland where they'll face one of the top defenses in the world."

Kaylee's ears perked up. "Too bad they're not playing Ireland tonight! Maybe they'd show some pictures of the countryside or—"

"Sh!" Jackie put a finger in front of her lips, her eyes riveted to the screen. "The game's starting!"

The ride to the early November feis in Chicago was as chilly as the outside weather. Caitlin hardly said a word. She did not come off as angry. She simply behaved as if Kaylee were not there.

At first, Kaylee tried acting as if a rift had never existed between them. Maybe Caitlin would be over it by now. After all, it was totally immature to be upset for this long simply because your friend had earned a few more first places than you had.

"This should be fun!" said Kaylee excitedly as she bounced into the seat next to Caitlin. "It's been awhile since we went to a feis together!"

Caitlin played with the zipper on the duffel bag in her lap and spoke with a tone usually reserved for reciting the answer to a particularly tedious math problem. "Yeah."

"I brought along rice cakes," said Kaylee brightly, patting the paper bag next to her. "Honey nut. The kind you like. Do you want one?"

Caitlin shook her head slowly, her eyes still on the zipper. "No."

Kaylee set the bag on the floor and thought for a moment before continuing. "I slept over at Jackie's last weekend. She was going crazy because we were watching Angelo Zizzo's first game back after an injury, and Jackie's an Angelo Zizzo fanatic. Then all she wanted to do was talk about the game and how great he was until two in the morning! Can you believe that?"

Caitlin answered once again in the math class voice. "Yeah."

Now Kaylee sat back in her seat with a frustrated sigh. She wanted to scream and tell her friend what a creep she was being, to tell her to get over it so things could get back to normal. Mrs. Hubbard seemed to sense the tension the way someone standing in the rain forest might sense the humidity. Kaylee could tell that she was working hard to find something to lighten the mood.

"Did you girls notice that we got one of those electronic toll passes?" she asked, pointing to a small white box near the rearview mirror. "Now we won't have to wait in line to pay tolls. Isn't that great?"

"Yeah," said both girls, their voices nearly petrified with math enthusiasm.

At the feis, the two families set up camp together, but after that, Kaylee and Caitlin seemed intent on staying out of each other's way as much as possible. Caitlin hung out with Meghan and April while Kaylee found Jordi and Hannah.

On her visits back to the camping area, Kaylee noticed the pained looks in her mother's and Mrs. Hubbard's eyes.

The reel was up first for Kaylee, but as she danced, something did not feel right. *Probably because I'm not used to competing in Open*, Kaylee thought. However, she knew the real reason probably had more to do with how frustrated and distracted this silly feud with Caitlin had made her.

She felt no better during her other dances.

*I don't care how I place today,* she thought. *I just hope Caitlin gets a ton of firsts. That'll put her in a better mood.*

And so she crossed her fingers late in the day as she made her way to the results area.

Fifth place in her hornpipe. Another fifth place in her reel.

*Guess I'm not exactly ready for the World Championships in Ireland.*

She was about to search for Caitlin's results when she caught sight of her friend—was that still the right word?—out of the corner of her eye. Instead, Kaylee circled back to the camp area where she began checking to make sure she had packed everything in her dress bag. The mothers were off somewhere, probably checking out the vendors. Finally Caitlin returned, sat in a folding chair, and began digging in her makeup kit. However, she said nothing. Silent minutes ticked by until Kaylee could scarcely stand it. She decided to take a chance.

"How did you do?"

Caitlin turned toward her, glaring, almost shocked, it seemed, that Kaylee had spoken to her. When she finally responded, her voice was as angry as her eyes. "How did I do?"

"Yeah," said Kaylee hesitantly, now wishing that she had remained quiet. "I was wondering if you had a good day."

"I had a really good day," said Caitlin, although she said it as if she meant just the opposite. "Two thirds."

"Two third places is pretty good," said Kaylee, although she knew immediately that this had not helped at all. In fact, it seemed to make things worse.

"Oh, yes," said Caitlin with exaggerated rancor. "Two thirds is just peachy and amazing for almost everybody. Especially if you happen to be in Open in everything. Then you can sit up there and look down on everybody else and think about how superior you are."

Kaylee blinked in surprise. "I don't think I'm superior."

"Oh sure," said Caitlin. "Then why are you hanging around with snobs like Brittany Hall?"

Kaylee's mouth dropped so wide that it took her a moment to respond. "Brittany Hall? She hates my guts!"

"That's not the way I heard it," said Caitlin, jabbing her makeup kit into her dress bag. "I heard you've been 'partying' at her house."

Kaylee could only guess how Caitlin had heard about the party. Perhaps Brittany had bragged to other dancers at Golden Academy about the raid and her escape from the law.

"I work hard and try to be the good girl," continued Caitlin, "while you party it up with a bunch of snobby millionaires."

Now Kaylee began to feel her anger rising. "Brittany's not a millionaire. Her father—" Kaylee stopped herself, wondering whether she should divulge private details about someone else's family—even if it were Brittany's.

"And the worst part is that you're still a better dancer than me!" said Caitlin, and her voice cracked a bit as she said this. She turned away, but her shoulders shook and Kaylee guessed she was crying.

Kaylee wanted to slip an arm around her friend, but she was certain Caitlin would only push her away. Caitlin jealousy had twisted her perspective, destroying their friendship, and Kaylee had no idea how to change things. She turned from the campsite and ran out through the vendor area, searching for someplace to hide, someplace where she could . . . cry? Scream? Explode? She found a spot near the food court on a bench partially hidden by a large potted plant. She sat with her head in her hands, not crying but rather feeling the deep pain that comes with not being able to change the world back to the way it was before. She knew she would have to go back to the camp area soon. Her mother and Mrs. Hubbard would want to leave now that the girls had finished their dances. But for now, Kaylee simply needed to sit. To let her breathing slow. To find the strength to deal with a long ride home in the company of someone who hated her.

And just as she felt herself gaining some control, she saw him.

Riley, the cute boy from Golden Academy, the boy who had come to meet her at the spring dance last year, who had stood close to her on the top deck of the ferry — there he was.

With someone else.

He sat across from a very cute girl in a dancer's wig, sweat pants and a feis t-shirt. They were sharing a cardboard nacho boat.

Kaylee dreaded the two-hour ride back to Rosemary, which she knew would be the longest two hours of her life. They turned out to be the longest two hours and forty-five minutes when they encountered a traffic jam near O'Hare airport.

"Chicago is just awful!" said Mrs. Hubbard as she inched along behind a furniture delivery truck.

"It sure is," muttered Kaylee. However, she was not talking about the traffic.

# *Twenty*

Thanksgiving felt very different. Mrs. O'Shay usually cooked a turkey with all the trimmings and great desserts and everyone ate way too much. This year, Mrs. O'Shay still cooked, but she prepared the dinner at Aunt Kat's apartment. Tom O'Shay set up a couple of folding tables and they crowded around to eat and count their blessings.

For the first time that Kaylee could remember, she did not feel very blessed. Yes, she had achieved one of her major goals the past year by moving into Open Prizewinner in all of her dances. But she seemed to have lost everything else important to her along the way.

Jackie seemed completely absorbed in soccer.

Caitlin hated her.

Riley was sharing nachos with someone else.

And then there was Aunt Kat. She looked as if she had aged ten years in the past month. Today, however, her energy seemed to have returned. She smiled, helped out in the kitchen, told stories about her life in Chicago and even laughed. Kaylee noticed, though, that Aunt Kat did not eat very much. Still, the day seemed almost normal most of the time.

Late in the afternoon, while her father sat watching a football game he had found on Aunt Kat's TV, while Will napped on the sofa, and while Kaylee's mother and Grandma Birdsall washed dishes in the kitchen, Aunt Kat led Kaylee into the bedroom. They sat on the bed and Aunt Kat wore a concerned look. "How are you doing, Munchkin?"

Kaylee could hardly believe the question. "How am *I* doing? I should be asking *you*!"

Aunt Kat smiled, bringing the old Aunt Kat into the room for an instant. "I heard you and Caitlin are still going through a rough period."

Kaylee almost laughed at the grossness of the understatement. A rough period? That made it sound like Kaylee were standing beneath a rain cloud that would soon pass, and then the sunny skies of friendship would be back complete with chirping birds and adorable talking forest animals. "I don't think it's a rough period. I think our friendship is basically over."

It was the first time she had said it, and the power of the words seemed to open the floodgates. Tears streamed down her cheeks and Aunt Kat gathered her in.

"Oh, sweetheart, don't be so quick to assume the worst. Relationships are just like everything else in life. Most of the time, things are wonderful, beautiful. But there are going to be tough times where it seems like everything is falling apart. Have faith. True friends may get lost for awhile, but they find their way back eventually."

Kaylee looked up, wiping her eyes. "How can you be so optimistic? After all you've been through?" Then Kaylee wondered whether this was something she should not have said. Aunt Kat did not seem to mind.

"Has the cancer been tough on me? You bet it has. It's been awful, and there have been days when I wondered whether I had the strength to go on. But you don't think I've given up, do you?"

Kaylee shook her head.

"Don't you give up, either," continued her aunt. "Not on your friends. And not on me. You'd be as bad as your mother."

"She hasn't given up on you, Aunt Kat," said Kaylee, surprised.

"Sometimes it seems like she has," said Aunt Kat shakily. "She can hardly bring herself to look at me. And she only talks to me to tell me that I'm overdoing it and I need to rest. Just the other day she said that maybe it wasn't such a good idea to take the trip to Ireland considering my 'condition'."

Kaylee's eyes widened. "We're still going, aren't we?"

A smile played at the corner of her aunt's lips. "Nothing in this world is going to stop me from getting on that plane."

Her aunt's determination gave Kaylee a boost. As she looked into her eyes, Kaylee knew that there was still an incredible reserve of energy within, and while it might take awhile, everything would ultimately be all right.

Kaylee wondered whether their meeting was at an end, but Aunt Kat reached to the bedside table and pulled her sketchbook into her lap.

"I was thinking," said Aunt Kat, "that I've got sketches of so many different dancers in here, but I've never sketched a picture of my favorite niece all by herself."

"I'm your only niece!"

Kat drew forth a pencil and opened the sketchbook. "Makes no difference. You're beautiful. For a munchkin. Now sit there nice. And smile!"

Smile. For the first time in quite awhile, Kaylee did.

The call came at three in the morning.

"When a telephone rings in the middle of the night, it's never good news," Kaylee's father always said.

The ring woke Kaylee, who leaned against her door jamb and listened. "That was mom," said Mrs. O'Shay shakily to her husband. She pulled on a sweatshirt and a jacket as she spoke. "She had to call an ambulance for Kat. I'm meeting her at the hospital in Paavo."

"Should I get dressed?" asked Mr. O'Shay.

Kaylee's mother shook her head. "Stay here with the kids. I'll call you when I know more."

As her mother headed for the door, Kaylee stepped out of her room. "Is Aunt Kat going to be okay?"

Her mother paused, but only for an instant. "I don't know, honey." And then she was out the door.

For the next two hours, Kaylee turned restlessly in her bed, unable to sleep, imagining the sorts of horrible things people imagine when loved ones are taken to the hospital in the middle of the night. Her father seemed to have gone back to bed, and Will had an almost superhuman ability to sleep through anything short of a bedside boat horn. No phone call came from her mother, and Kaylee could not decide whether this was a good or bad thing. Just after five, she drifted off to a fitful and unsatisfying sleep, but she woke an hour later to the sound of the kitchen door.

"Mom?" Kaylee had come to her doorway and stood watching her mother drape her coat over a kitchen chair.

Mrs. O'Shay put her index finger to her lips and quietly crossed the living room. As her features became more clear in the dim light, Kaylee saw how weary Bethany O'Shay looked.

"How's Aunt Kat?"

Her mother shepherded Kaylee to the bed and sat beside her. "She's not doing well, Kaylee." And then she amended this. "Pretty bad."

This frightened Kaylee. Her mother had previously avoided any direct reference to Aunt Kat's condition, especially anything negative, as if she might be able to will it away by ignoring it. Apparently the time for that had passed.

"Is she going to have to have surgery?"

Bethany O'Shay took a moment, as if to steel herself against the impact of her next words. "Aunt Kat is dying," she said with surprising softness, slipping an arm around her daughter's shoulders.

A tear ran silently down Kaylee's cheek. She was surprised that the news did not hit her with more force, did not reduce her to a wailing heap of reddish-brown curls and salt water. Somehow, it seemed she had known this for awhile.

"She might have a couple of months," continued her mother. "It depends on . . . a lot of things."

They sat holding each other for a long time.

# Twenty-one

The days leading up to Christmas break were usually a blur of bright whites and greens and reds, happy smiles and expectations. For Kaylee, everything seemed to be a slush-gray soup that soaked to her core. Her world reverberated with loss: Caitlin, Riley, Aunt Kat. And Jackie seemed so busy with her own classes and the start of indoor soccer that she might as well have lived on the opposite side of the planet.

Evenings meant homework and a trip to Aunt Kat's apartment. After a week in the Paavo hospital, she had been sent home. Now, however, she spent most of her days in bed. An attendant from a hospice spent several hours each day at Aunt Kat's helping out, since Grandma Birdsall was no longer able to handle the care alone. Conversations were difficult. Each evening the same questions about work and school and soccer and dance seemed to replay themselves. All they could talk about, it seemed, was the past. To make conversation about the future—a future Aunt Kat would probably never see-- seemed almost obscene.

One evening when everyone else had somehow drifted into the kitchen, Aunt Kat found herself alone with Kaylee in the living room and deviated from the script.

"Sorry about messing everything up, Munchkin," she said.

Kaylee gazed at her aunt's hands. They looked nearly normal, and so she could almost imagine that the woman she was talking with was not completely bald with tubes running from her nose and left arm. "Aunt Kat, you didn't mess anything up! You did everything right! You ate the right foods, you exercised. Even after you were diagnosed, you never gave up. You were always so positive. It's just not fair!"

Aunt Kat squeezed one of Kaylee's hands. "Yeah, I know. The hardest part is knowing that there's a guy out there eating doughnuts for breakfast every morning and he's going to live to be a hundred."

"You've worked so hard to beat this," said Kaylee. "I thought that if you tried your hardest, you could do anything!"

"If you try your hardest, you can do amazing things," Aunt Kat corrected her.

"Keep your eye on the top of the mountain," whispered Kaylee.

Aunt Kat mustered a tired smile. "That's where I've always kept mine. But not everyone reaches the top, you know."

Kaylee sniffed to keep the tears away. "Then why even try?"

"Because," said her aunt, "the view keeps getting better the higher you climb."

Kaylee hesitated, and this time a tear did slide down her cheek. "I just wish we could climb together."

Aunt Kat slipped an arm around her shoulders. "Just keep climbing, Munchkin. No matter how high you climb, you won't be alone."

Kaylee wiped her eye with the back of her hand. Aunt Kat took the opportunity to reach to the bedside table and grab her sketch book.

"This seems like as good a time as any to give you this."

Kaylee's mouth fell open slightly as she took the book. "Me? Your sketch book?"

"It's my present to you. I told you that I wanted to give it to you. Merry Christmas. Just a bit early."

Kaylee flipped through the sketchbook quickly. "But there are still plenty of blank pages left."

Aunt Kat leaned back on her pillow, closing her eyes. "It's finished," she said softly.

Now Kaylee examined the book more closely. It had a worn, tan cover and was bound at the top so that the pages could be flipped over as each new sketch was completed. About two-thirds of the booklet seemed to have been filled with about forty sketches. Most were beautiful renderings of dancers in school or solo costumes. The last drawing, however, was a portrait of Kaylee that Aunt Kat had created in that very room just a couple of weeks earlier.

"They're beautiful, Aunt Kat," said Kaylee, paging backward toward the beginning of the book. As she came to the half a dozen sketches nearest the front, the subject matter suddenly changed. Instead of dancers, there were sketches of a house, people sitting underneath a tree, and a boat on a lake among others. Sandwiched in between these was one more Irish dancer, and this one was the most beautiful of all. Using colored pencils, her Aunt Kat had drawn a picture of Kaylee in a gorgeous green solo dress, the sort of dress that Kaylee had dreamed about. "Wow," murmured Kaylee, hardly able to take her eyes off the amazing work.  Then she flipped back to the portrait of herself at the end of the book.  "But I thought you said you hadn't done any other sketches of me."

She lowered the book and noticed that her aunt had fallen asleep.

Her parents, Will and Grandma Birdsall returned from the kitchen and found seats.

"Sleeping again," said Grandma Birdsall, caressing Aunt Kat's forehead with a hand.  "Poor dear."

Bethany O'Shay watched her sister sleep for a minute.  "Do you think she'll be okay while we're gone?"

"A woman from the hospice will be staying here 24-7," said Tom O'Shay.

"And I'll be staying, too," noted Grandma Birdsall.

Kaylee looked around at the adults, just beginning to understand.  "Aunt Kat's not going to Ireland?"

Bethany O'Shay smiled wanly.  "She's in no condition to make the trip, honey.  But she really wanted us to go.  Especially you."

Kaylee's eyes dropped to the floor.  "She was really looking forward to going.  She wanted to hear the music.  See the green hills."

"I know," said her mother.  "We'll have to bring back plenty of pictures and stories."

Kaylee looked directly at her aunt now, and then her eyes raced around the room.  *Never give up.  Keep your eyes on the top of the mountain.*  "There must be some way.  She could use a wheelchair!  They allow wheelchairs on planes, don't they?  And maybe a nurse could come with us!  And I could help give Aunt Kat her medicines and feed her!"

Mrs. O'Shay gazed lovingly at her daughter. "Kaylee, you're sweet. And nothing would make me happier. But she just can't."

Her father nodded in agreement. "Sorry sweetheart."

Now Kaylee felt truly helpless. She had worked hard and had made the Open level in all of her dances. But she could not make her aunt better. No matter what she did, no matter how hard she tried.

There was no way Aunt Kat would be spending Christmas in Ireland.

# Twenty-two

Every eighth grader was required to take chorus, and this meant that every eighth grader would be participating in the Kennedy Park Middle School Christmas concert three days before the start of the holiday break. As far as Kaylee was concerned, these were the sort of awful events that inevitably occurred when schools entertained the fiction that all people could be taught to produce reasonably acceptable music.

The event became even more awful when Kaylee failed to find her parents or Will in the audience. They always sat next to the Kizobus, and although Kaylee found Jackie's parents in the fifth row of folding chairs, she saw no sign of her own.

There were probably a hundred reasonable explanations for their absence. Only one, however, was on Kaylee's mind: Aunt Kat.

"She's back in the hospital," said Tom O'Shay when he arrived to pick his daughter up after concert. "It's pretty bad."

At the hospital, Aunt Kat drifted in and out of sleep, barely aware of their presence, tubes protruding from everywhere, it seemed. Grandma Birdsall sat beside her holding one of Kat's hands. After midnight, Tom

O'Shay drove home with his children, leaving Grandma Birdsall and Mrs. O'Shay behind.

Kaylee fell asleep in two classes the next day.

At the hospital that evening, Aunt Kat woke occasionally but talked little. "She knows we're all here," said Grandma Birdsall. "That's what's important."

The most incredible aspect of Aunt Kat's illness seemed to be Grandma Birdsall's response to it. This old woman with heart problems had barely been able to take care of herself before. However, she seemed to find some extra energy reserve to do whatever needed to be done for Aunt Kat. At home, Grandma Birdsall had seemed unable to remain awake for more than two or three hours at a time, but she sat at Aunt Kat's bedside without a yawn, like a sentinel at the gate to the fortress.

A doctor or nurse would occasionally speak with Mrs. O'Shay. Kaylee never heard a word of these conversations, yet she understood them completely. She could read their eyes, the slope of their shoulders, the tightness at the corners of the mouths.

And she knew without having to ask that none of them would be spending Christmas in Ireland.

On Christmas Eve, Kaylee slept in until almost noon. There had been no time to put up decorations or even get a tree, and so Kaylee and Will used the afternoon hours to dig through the boxes in their basement and create a tiny bit of holiday atmosphere. They even dug out the old artificial Christmas tree which they had not used in four years.

Kaylee did not look forward to the coming hours in the dreary hospital room, yet she did not look forward to that day in the very near future when those hours would abruptly come to an end. Christmas was supposed to be a time filled with joy and miracles, yet this year, everything felt wrong.

After supper, Tom O'Shay drove his children to Paavo. As they walked down the long hallway to Aunt Kat's room, Kaylee prayed for a miracle—as she always did. But this time she prayed even more fervently.

*Oh, please. It's Christmas Eve. Isn't that when miracles are supposed to occur?*

They passed the nurse's station. A tiny decorated tree sat on the counter.

*The perfect time. Just one little miracle.*

Her father pushed open the door to Aunt Kat's room, and Kaylee blinked, hardly able to believe what she was seeing.

She was in Ireland.

It was not really Ireland, of course, but the room had been transformed. Irish fiddle music jounced from a CD player in a corner of the room. A crock pot sat on a low table, and from it came the rich smell of stew. The walls were nearly covered with dozens of posters of Irish landmarks and of the beautiful emerald countryside. Jackie turned from where she was taping one of the last of the posters into place and smiled at Kaylee.

"Posterbeast," she grinned, waving at the wall.

Several others who had been helping to hang the posters now turned away from the wall: Jordi, Hannah, April, Meghan . . . and Riley. They were all here. All in their Irish dance costumes.

Kaylee found herself consumed in hugs.

"But," said Kaylee as she recovered her voice, "I thought this part of the hospital only allowed family members."

"I have lots of children today," said Mrs. O'Shay, and Kaylee could see from the look on her face that no nurse would think to challenge her.

Kaylee gazed around the room, trying to take it all in. "But . . . how?"

"We just wanted to do something to help," said Hannah. Jordi nodded in agreement. "But it was Jackie and Caitlin who organized everything."

Kaylee blinked. "Caitlin?"

As if on cue, the bathroom door swung open and Caitlin, adjusting her solo dress, stepped out. Kaylee rushed to hug her, and now the tears streamed down her face. "Why don't you change into your dress?" said Caitlin when they finally parted.

"My dance dress?" asked Kaylee. "It's at home."

Mrs. O'Shay lifted the dress bag off the back of the chair nearest Aunt Kat's bed. "Your dad dropped it off here this morning before you woke up."

Kaylee rushed to the bathroom and made the quickest change in solo dress history. "What now?" she asked.

"Does your aunt have a favorite dance?" asked Riley.

Kaylee nodded. "She likes the hard shoe dances best."

Jackie cued up the hornpipe music and they danced, their footsteps echoing like winter thunder off the tile floor.

They were in Ireland.

They danced and Aunt Kat watched, smiling, unable to speak, yet saying everything with her smile.

This was love. This was life. This, Kaylee O'Shay decided, was where she belonged.

## Kaylee O'Shay, Irish Dancer
*Book Five: The Secret Ceili*

In her fifth year as a dancer, fourteen-year-old Kaylee O'Shay is chosen to dance on a ceili team for the Oireachtas. Kaylee knows that training for the big event will require hard work, sacrifice and cooperation. But are all eight of her ceili teammates willing to make the necessary commitment? Is Kaylee?

For more information about the Kaylee O'Shay series, visit the official online site at www.kayleeoshay.com.

## *Acknowledgements*

Thanks to My Lovely Wife Marsha, my greatest fan, friend and passion.

Thanks to my daughter, Haley Marie, whose editing helps me to bring Kaylee's world to life.  I am so proud of you.

Thanks to Alicia Strackbein, whose poem "Dance" is published at the beginning of this book with her permission.  The first time I read the poem, my reaction was "Wow!" and I knew it would be perfect for this book.

Thank you to everyone who helped in ways big and small.  Even if you were not named here, please know that I am enormously grateful for your contributions.

## *About the Author*

Rod Vick has written for newspapers and magazines, has worked as an editor and has taught writing workshops and classes over the span of a quarter century. His short stories have appeared in a variety of literary magazines and have won both regional and national awards. He has written twelve books that have become favorites of Irish dancers of all ages.

Rod Vick lives in Mukwonago, Wisconsin with his wife, Marsha, and children Haley and Joshua. An occasional speaker at conferences and orientation events, he also runs marathons, enthusiastically supports his children's dance and soccer passions, and pitches a pretty mean horseshoe.

Made in United States
North Haven, CT
17 December 2022

29516565R00112